CN00319699

THE
SURGEON

SALMAN WAQAR

Prologue

He feels a shiver run down his body as the cold anaesthetic gel is applied to his forearm. The sharp needle breaks skin, finds a vein, and the dark flush of blood on the plastic tip outside indicates it's in the right place. His mind tells him he must feel pain, but the gel has done its job and there is none. A plastic tube slides over the needle, resting on one end in his blood stream, like an eel in water, while the other is secured to the skin outside. This cannula, and a few others like it, will form a conduit for medicines to be pumped directly into his body.

Lying flat on his back in a small rectangular room, he glimpses cupboards and drawers filled with colour coded medicine boxes and vials. Beyond his feet, an automatic door stands guard between him and the operating theatre. Through its frosted glass, he can see silhouettes of nurses in green scrubs, getting ready for the hours ahead, and standing in the middle of the room an articulated structure, twice the height of the nurses, crouched on itself like a snake about to uncoil.

A man in blue scrubs is standing next to him, his hands holding vials of Fentanyl, Midazolam, Rocuronium and Propofol.

Together these will induce loss of response to pain, loss of memory, immobility, unconsciousness and muscle relaxation; the hallmarks of general anaesthesia.

"Also the same medicines used for euthanasia" he thinks, unable to escape the irony of it. Trying to keep his mind distracted, he thinks of the many herculean tasks to face, and difficult decisions to be made, in the days to come.

"At least this will be one less thing to worry about" he reassures himself.

The man turns around, places an oxygen mask on his face, and begins to inject the medicines into his vein.

"Don't worry, it'll be over before you know it" he says, as they start to take effect and his face begins to fade away.

Chapter One

January 16th, 2030.

"All is well, just closing up now Professor Ash" Rick looks up to the viewing gallery above the operating theatre, and nods his head.

Standing in the window is Professor Daniyaal Ashraf, known as Dan or Professor Ash to his friends and colleagues. He looks down at the operating theatre below. His registrar Rick is performing a routine appendicectomy and all is going as planned. The inflamed appendix has been successfully removed, and the incision is being closed, with Rick's well-trained hands approximating all the layers correctly. A white, shadow free, light glares down from the ceiling-mounted lamps, illuminating the green drapes that cover the patients' abdomen and creating a clean area to operate in. At the head of the patient stands the anaesthetist in her blue scrubs, keeping a close watch on his observations. "Obs" for short, these flicker across a touch screen monitor telling her how well the patient is breathing, his heart rate, blood pressure and a host of other data. She put him to sleep, will wake him up again after the surgery, and is responsible for keeping him alive in between. A nurse diligently hands and takes away instruments from Rick while another helps her as a "runner", keeping track of all the instruments being used, coding them onto a computer so it can auto-order if they are running low, and rushing around for any extra equipment that is required. In one corner, three hinged vents periodically flutter with the laminar flow system, allowing air to flow only in one direction, from the ceiling into the theatre and out through the vents, preventing any undesirable bacteria from gaining entry to the operating area.

"After all these years, there is still an element of awe watching this well oiled machine function. Maybe because with experience surgeons begin to appreciate how surgery is an art as much as it is a disciplined system" Dan thinks as he looks at his reflection in the viewing glass.

"A few wrinkles – maybe a bit more than a few, gelled back silver hair, tight jawline and a strong, lean build. Not too bad for someone about to retire" he smiles to himself.

Retirement reminds him of how far he has progressed in his parents adopted homeland. The son of Pakistani immigrants, his privileged upbringing was an excellent headstart. The only son of a father who was a commercial airline pilot and a mother who is a chef, he went to the best school in town and graduated in medicine from Imperial College, London. Once he found his passion, first in General and later in Cardiothoracic surgery, he pursued it with relentless energy and dedication.

"I'm done, Professor Ash" says Rick as he applies the last surgical staple to the patient's skin and stretches his shoulders.

Dan chuckles to himself as he remembers his father, who could never figure out why people wanted to shorten names "What's wrong with simply calling you Daniyaal or Professor Ashraf? It's short enough as it is! Why shorten it further to Dan or Ash?"

He nods his head in approval.

"Well done Rick. You have done enough of these now to feel confident converting to open surgery, if things are not going to plan with minimally invasive techniques."

As a promising surgeon he had risen through the ranks quickly. In his career he had seen a massive evolution in the practise of surgery. Initially, many years had been spent mastering the art of operating through large incisions, followed by learning small incision surgery, up until the era of minimally invasive laparoscopic surgery- different instruments and cameras inserted into the body via strategically placed micro incisions, used to perform all kinds of surgical procedures. Each evolution had taken considerable retraining and he was proud that he had always been at the fore front. And now there is robotic surgery –

"Part of me wishes I had more time to explore the new frontier. But perhaps winding down is the wise thing to do" he concludes.

His impending retirement had recently boosted his popularity as a "teacher of the old ways". The past six months had been spent teaching open surgical techniques to as many as possible.

Sometimes the very basics are the only logical options in complicated situations.

Looking around the viewing gallery, there is no one there but him. It used to be packed with trainees and senior surgeons looking to learn from the operation happening in the "operating theatre", an ode to the very first surgical procedures performed in front of live audiences in an "amphitheatre". Nowadays a live video of the surgery is simply sent to various television screens in the staffs sitting area, and to the surgical teams' electronic devices.

He could have seen Rick operating on his computer in the comfort of his office, "But I do enjoy my occasional trip to this gallery, brings back so many memories."

He gets up to leave, thinking of the rest of his schedule for the day and looking forward to ending it with a long run, in preparation for his fourth marathon.

"Although it seems age is slowly creeping up on me, threatening to slow me down" he muses, hearing his knees crackle as he stands up and reaches for the intercom.

"Rick will you be joining me for a ward round in the evening?"

"Negative Professor" Rick responds "I have to clock out at six so will be handing over to Josh who will join you".

"Please make sure he is on the ball with all our patients and thanks for your help during the day"

Rick replies with a thumbs up as he moves out of the theatre to unscrub.

Walking out, Daniyaal thinks about the way things have changed in the National Health Service during his career.

"Clocking out at six; wouldn't that have been a treat back in my time."

Daniyaal's training was during the time of thirty six hour shifts with twelve hour breaks. Doctors were expected to work such hours that the hospital would become their first home. And whilst the working patterns of his early years afforded better continuity of care for the patients, and a greater sense of belonging to a team for the doctors, the price to pay was soon too high to ignore. There was an ocean of files in the General Medical Council that archived the careers of brilliant minds lost to lawsuits over malpractice. Many of the professor's colleagues lost their medical licenses over missed diagnoses and incorrect prescribing. The press always had their versions, but he knew the majority had buckled either under the strain of sleep deprivation or the constant onslaught of stress brought on by trying to keep their personal lives afloat.

"In hindsight, I was very lucky to make it through training without a blemish."

After years of living the expected status quo, later on as a consultant, he earned the flexibility and had gained the wisdom to actively work towards a better work-life balance, and spend more time with his wife and daughter. The introduction of the European Working Time Directive in the early twenty first century then made it possible to achieve this balance from the very beginning of training, limiting working hours to a maximum of forty eight per week.

"A change for the better." he thinks "although it is nice sometimes to have the power to jest with trainees about how they are not as hardy as my generation was."

After the United Kingdom opted in the twenty sixteen referendum to leave the European Union, this was replaced by a national directive but the principal remained the same. Doctor errors due to fatigue reduced dramatically, and for working hours to remain compliant, shift patterns were adopted. This initially resulted in lack of continuity of care for patients and had some negative consequences, but the NHS was quick to adapt, and now well organised handover meetings at the change of each shift ensure streamlined, good quality patient care.

He walks slowly up the generic NHS staircase. Easy to clean floor matting with a hand rail on one side, and a bar on the wall in case someone needs extra support. Colourful boards highlight each floor as he ascends, smiling as he always does at the one on the paediatric ward floor. A boy in a space suit is making a figure of six with his jetpack. It reminds him of a cartoon he used to watch with his daughter when she was younger.

"Those days are in the past now. She will be a fully qualified marine biologist soon. How time flies."

He exits the stair way on the seventh floor and walks down the corridor to his office, punching in the correct number onto the keypad to enter. It is a small office which he shares with his friend and fellow surgeon, James. On his many visits to hospitals in the United States, Daniyaal has always been struck by how lavish their offices are. But the size of his office has never bothered him much.

It is yet another example of the NHS ethos – effective utilisation of space and resources, making sure the whole institution benefits as much as possible.

He sits down at his desk with a mug of coffee.

"Advances in surgery." he reads off the screen.

"Right then, let's see if I can make this presentation exciting for the hundred medical students who are going to be staring at me tomorrow"

"Ready for the ward round Professor" Josh announces an hour later, as he knocks on his door, just as Daniyaal is about to log off.

"Be with you in two minutes" he answers, turning off the computer.

Chapter Two

Daniyaal walks in, smartly dressed in a black suit, sky blue shirt, a tie with the Royal College emblem and his favourite Star Wars socks, which are a vital part of all important lectures.

Familiar faces descend down the rows of the lecture theatre. Some alert, some distracted, some just exhausted; they all wait for him to start.

"I am Daniyaal Ashraf, and I can see that not all of you have had enough coffee this morning."

Nervous laughter echoes in the room.

"But I can also see that regardless of whether you look like a ray of sunshine or worn out by the rigors of medical school, you all share an aura of determination to master the art and science of medicine and surgery. And that is fantastic."

Most of them sit up straighter now, and their expressions generally relax a bit.

"No harm in helping budding doctors believe they have that 'extra something'" he thinks to himself.

He takes the medical students through a fascinating journey, starting from the days before the development of anaesthesia in the mid nineteenth and antibiotics in the early twentieth century. They quickly progress to images and videos of open surgical procedures using large incisions, laparoscopic surgery and then finally robotic surgery.

"The development of robotic surgery is one of the most important advances in surgery in this century."

"The story goes as so. In the late twentieth century, various teams in the United States of America began working on the concept of assisting surgery via robotics. The initial funding and research was done by the National Aeronautical and Space Agency and the Defence Advanced Research Projects Agency, via grants to different universities. NASAs Ames Research group was interested in a way to conduct remote surgery for its astronauts on the International Space Station. The idea was that the surgeon would be based on Earth and a robotic system on the ISS would be linked up to him. Separately, the US Military had long been aware that many of its troops in conflict zones exsanguinated before they could be transferred to a major trauma centre, so DARPA also invested heavily in research to develop robotic systems that could be deployed on the battlefield, treating the soldier on site, with a surgeon remotely controlling the robot."

Daniyaal swipes the screen on his watch and moves to the next slide.

"Initial models included simple, single armed, robots used for precision brain tissue biopsies in neurosurgery, and to accurately shape the head of the femoral bone for hip replacements. Many different iterations followed but soon one institute got ahead of the pack. A team at the Stanford Research Institute developed the first true robotic surgery system."

He points to a slide showcasing the early system. It shows a surgeon sitting at a console in one corner of the theatre. In each hand he holds a master controller with finger grips that allow his movements to be translated to movements of the robotic arms. Under his feet are various control pedals and in front of him is a viewing screen, projecting a 3D image of the operating field. Above the patient are three robotic arms ready to be inserted into the abdomen. These are multi articulated with small probes at their tips, which can be moved in all the directions a human wrist can. One arm has a light source and a camera whilst the others house the surgical instruments.

"This early system was commercialised by Synchrony Robotics Inc and of course has now been developed further to its current form of single incision robotic surgery."

Heads nod in the audience as a wave of recognition goes across the hall. Everyone has heard of Synchrony Robotics Inc. The world leader in robotics, they are not only the dominant company in surgical but also space, industrial and military robotics. Nearly every surgical theatre in the NHS now has one of their systems installed. It is of much interest to the audience that they had their humble beginnings in surgery.

He moves to the next slide which shows the latest cardiothoracic robotics system. The surgeon again sits on one side of the theatre but this time she is wearing a chic virtual reality headset with smart looking gloves on her hands, which seamlessly turn into sleeves that run up her forearms and to her shoulders. These have spatial detectors in them, which are able to translate her movements with extreme accuracy to the robotic system. Attached to the surgical bed is a single robotic arm. It is covered in a black mesh but a slit in this shows interconnected concentric rings of composite alloy, that allow it to move in any direction needed. At its tip are multiple holes from which emerge a wide array of smaller arms but with a similar construction, each fitted with a different surgical instrument and capable of similar snake like agility.

"This is where we are at present. Robotic systems have improved surgical outcomes by utilising a single small incision, increasing surgeon accuracy, allowing intra operative real time diagnostic imaging to guide treatment and by enabling telesurgery, whereby surgical expertise can be transmitted across the world to developing areas who may not have it."

"The future however is even brighter with the development of A.I.R, but that is something we will discuss in my next lecture. Thank you for your time" Daniyaal smiles at the audience, turning the projector off.

Leaving the stage he feels his watch vibrate, indicating he has received an email. Looking at it as he walks out of the lecture theatre, he sees it's from Gary Richards. He had gone to medical school with Daniyaal and they had completed most of their surgical training together. Gary, however, had later found his interest in medico-legal proceedings and now works for the GMC investigating complex surgical complaints.

{Hi Daniyaal,

Sorry it's been a while but you know how things can be at the GMC. I need to speak to you urgently. Any chance you can drop by my office sometime today?

Best

Gary}

"Well that's a surprise! I can't think of many circumstances in which Gary would ask for help."

{No problem – will be there in about 20 minutes} Daniyaal dictates to his watch.

As he hears the distinctive whooshing sound which tells him the email has been sent, he wonders what has the GMC and Gary so worried.

Chapter Three

A short walk to Holborn Underground Station, the Piccadilly Line to Kings Cross and then onto the Circle Line, heading to Great Portland Street Station. Daniyaal steps out of the station into the light rain and begins walking up Euston Road. The tall glass building of the General Medical Council looms high on his right. A large sign frames the main entrance with the GMCs motto: "Working with doctors, working for patients".

He enters the building and is glad to be out of the rain.

"Good afternoon. How can I help you?" asks the young receptionist.

"I'm here to see Gary Richards please. He is expecting me" he replies.

"Not a problem. Head up the elevator to level four. Turn right as you get off. His office is at the end of the corridor" she says, pointing to an elevator to her left.

Formed in 1858, the GMC is a public body that maintains the official register of medical practitioners within the United

Kingdom. Its chief responsibility is to protect, promote and maintain the health and safety of the public, by controlling entry to the register, and suspending or removing members when necessary. The GMC also sets the standards for medical schools in the U.K. More recently it has been in charge of revalidating doctors as fit to practice every five years.

An automated voice chimes "Level four" and the doors open. Daniyaal steps out, turns right.

Gary is standing outside his office, waiting for him.

"Good to see you again buddy" he says enthusiastically as he gives him a strong hand shake. With his fair skin, red hair and freckled face, his boyish looks have not changed in many years.

Daniyaal smiles. During his training, Gary had joined the Territorial Army before moving to the GMC. He had been deployed once on a peace keeping mission to Somalia, and once to Afghanistan. Since then the military mannerisms of a crisp handshake and getting straight to the point in a conversation had not left him.

"Come on in" Gary opens the door and they walk in.

"Nice office" Daniyaal quips "Larger than my NHS one".

Gary is now head of the Complex Complaints Team and has a corner office with a large wall size window on one side, offering a sweeping view of the city.

"It is posh, isn't it! Thanks for coming over" he replies, sitting down on his worn out leather office chair.

"You know I'm always happy to help" Daniyaal looks at the double decker buses moving along their routes on Euston Road below.

"It's been too long since we met up for a good chat" Gary says, smiling at him "We should definitely plan to get the families together one of these days, perhaps when we are both retired?"

"That would be nice. Last time I saw you, you were climbing into a military jeep headed for god knows where." Meeting Gary again has brought back a flood of memories from their time together in training. The many shifts spent together on the wards, countless lives saved, and some lost, laying the foundations of a strong bond that has not weakened despite the separation of time.

"You know I can't talk about that!" Gary says, with a quick wink and a lopsided grin. "But I do have something else that will catch your interest. You know what my team does, right?"

"You're tasked with investigating complicated cases of medical negligence, after a doctor has been reported to the GMC's fitness to practice panel" Daniyaal answers, taking a seat.

"Precisely! So imagine my surprise when I received a call from my boss, instructing me to assist Scotland Yard with a case that hasn't even been referred to the GMC yet!"

"That sounds unusual" Daniyaal agrees.

"Have you heard of Samuel Briffa?" Gary continues.

Daniyaal shakes his head.

"Neither had I until today. He is a Member of Parliament from Sheffield for the Conservative Party. He underwent routine Coronary Artery Bypass Grafting in his city yesterday. Only things didn't go as planned and he died during surgery."

"That's very unusual! CABG is a very routine and safe procedure now. With single incision robotic systems, patients go home the same day and mortality is almost unheard off" Daniyaal remarks "Who was the surgeon?"

"Mr Alex Chang"

Daniyaal wipes some rain droplets of his trousers as he tries to recall the name. He does not know Chang personally but has met him formally at various conferences. "Chang is good and has many years of experience with robotic CABG. But before we discuss him, why is Scotland Yard interested in this case? I've never heard of them investigating medical negligence cases."

"The surgical records indicate Mr Chang perforated the heart wall during surgery. Briffa bled to death on-table before the anaesthetist even realised what had happened." Gary looks at Daniyaal, with an expression of scepticism.

"That's impossible." Daniyaal sits up straight "Not with the robotic systems and certainly not with A.I.R watching!"

"That's exactly what Scotland Yard is concerned about. The case is high profile because Briffa was close to Prime Minister Edwards, and it's not going to be long before the media gets hold of the news. For this to happen with a robotics system and A.I.R oversight raises many concerns, most important of which is that the act was not possible without prior planning. They are going to treat it as homicide unless proven otherwise, and want someone from the GMC to assist them. I don't have anyone with the required expertise so have put your name forward."

"But I'm about to retire!" Daniyaal inhales sharply "You should've asked me first."

"Don't tell me this doesn't intrigue you. You've spent a lifetime performing surgery and training surgeons. Aren't you even a little curious about what happened?"

He thinks about his plans. The official retirement date is in two days time. His wife, Zaynab, is away on an interior design course to Italy for a month and his daughter, Aalia, is tied up with studies in university.

"Gary is right. Whether it is proven to be homicide or negligence, either way, the implications for surgeons and their patients are going to be enormous, and I do have the expertise to offer." Daniyaal weighs things in his head.

"I suppose Rick could cover my routine clinics for the next two days" He finally says, looking at the ceiling above.

"Fantastic! There is no time to waste. We need to get you to Scotland Yard for a briefing straight away." Gary jumps out of his seat, and they go out the door to head towards the elevator.

Outside the rain picks up as dark clouds announce their supremacy over the skies of the city.

Chapter Four

They get out at Westminster Tube Station. In front of them Big Ben stands tall and proud, as it has done for nearly two hundred years.

Walking under their umbrellas on Victoria Street, Daniyaal asks "Scotland Yard only investigates cases within the Greater London Area right?"

"Correct" replies Gary.

"The obvious question then is, why are they interested in investigating a suspected murder in Sheffield?" Daniyaal points out.

Gary presses the walk button as they stop at a pelican crossing. "Such is the new world of policing. The case is in Sheffield but Synchrony Robotics Inc and NHS Intellect are both based within the London area."

They cross the road at the green light.

"The worlds of medical regulation and law enforcement have developed many blurred lines in the last few years. With robotic systems and cybercrime, it is not always clear where jurisdiction lies, as there may be many players involved at different locations. I suspect in this case though, the Prime Minister might have made a personal request to Scotland Yard for help."

Gary and Daniyaal continue their journey, picking up the pace to try and get out of the rain as quickly as possible.

The development of robotic systems in surgery had created many legal dilemmas. In the initial years there had been many cases where surgeons stated that the robotic system had not translated their movements as intended, leading to harm to the patient. In such cases it often took a very thorough analysis of the robotic systems data to ascertain if it was the systems fault, or if the surgeon had indeed made a mistake and was transferring blame to the robot. Cases under investigation for medical negligence thus became joint investigative efforts between medical professionals and robotic engineers provided by Synchrony Robotics.

Furthermore, Telerobotics had its own unique issues. As the surgeon was remote to the operation site, any drop in connectivity between the two sites could be dangerous and some cases had suffered because of this. Robotic companies had circumvented this problem by ensuring backup systems on site, with a surgeon on standby, to stabilise things until connectivity returned, but this was not always easy to organise. The question asked in such cases was whether the telecommunication company involved in providing support was at fault, and this had led to a few litigations. Some telecom companies as a result stopped supporting telesurgical procedures altogether.

"Here we are" Gary points to a 1930's neo-classical building in front of them. It is eight stories high with multiple square windows, framed by thick slabs of concrete, on each floor. Outside revolves the iconic three sided sign with "New Scotland Yard" written on each face. The entrance is a large glass pavilion and an automatic door slides open as they approach. Gary leads Daniyaal to an elevator and punches the button for the seventh floor. He has obviously been here before and is expected today too.

On the seventh floor they enter a small, well-lit, conference room with an oval table in the centre, and a large screen on one wall.

"She should be here shortly" he says, pouring some water out of a jug on one side of the table.

They take a seat. Daniyaal checks his emails while they wait, and Gary brings up the British Broadcasting Corporation website to see if the news has broken yet.

"I am so sorry to keep you waiting" says a woman in her mid thirties as she walks in. She is dressed smartly in black trousers, a white blouse, black jacket and comfortable pumps. Her green eyes, high cheek bones, blonde hair and good posture betray an eastern european heritage.

"Tanya Kowalski, I work with Homicide" she smiles and extends her hand to Daniyaal. "I am sure you gentleman will remember how it is when you have young kids. I had a feeling this case would keep us busy for a while, so I had to arrange for my husband to pick them up after school."

Daniyaal smiles and passes Gary a knowing look. They sit down. Tanya taps her watch to dim the room lights and turn the wall screen on. She then makes a swiping motion from the watch to the screen, and a file floats on to it, giving the impression of data being transferred. The file opens, and pictures of two men, side by side, come into focus.

"The gentleman on the right is Mr Alex Chang. As you know, he is a Cardiothoracic Surgeon at Northern General Hospital, Sheffield. Born in Mauritius to Chinese parents, he got admission into medical school in Oxford and graduated with honours. He is well respected within the medical community for both his commitment to his patients and his clinical expertise. I am sure this is not new information for you, Professor Ashraf." Tanya begins.

"Please call me Dan" he says "And yes, I agree, his credentials are impeccable"

"He has been married for twenty years and has a son and daughter. His family suffered a terrible tragedy two years ago when his son was involved in a car crash which has left him paraplegic." she continues "His revalidation reports and appraisals however have not shown that this has impacted on his professional behaviour in any way. His surgical success rates remain one of the best in the country, and Mr Briffa had specifically requested his cardiologist for a referral to Mr Chang for his surgery. He is active with various medical research organisations, professional societies and charities, but none which flag up as a cause for concern."

Tanya points to the picture on the left. It is of a man in his fifties shaking hands with the Prime Minister. The picture has been taken at a white tie event. He is well turned out, with his thinning grey hair combed back and a large smile revealing polished teeth. He has a glint in his eyes which betrays both loyalty to the cause of his party, but also independent thinking.

"This is Samuel Briffa. He was born and raised in Sheffield. He joined the Conservative Party as a young man in his early twenties, about the same time as the PM, and they rose through the ranks of the party quickly. He received a lot of praise for the work he did over the years in his constituency, and the voters rewarded this by re-electing him continuously for fifteen years. He worked with the PM on various commissions and they did not always see eye to eye. Nonetheless they remained close, and he is very concerned about the news of Briffas death in such circumstances."

Tanya takes a sip of water.

"Two years ago he divorced from his wife after being married for twenty three years. They have one daughter, who is in University, and would split her time between them. Now I do not presume to understand the technical details of his medical history, so Gary would you mind taking over?"

"Sure thing" Gary sits up in his chair "Simply put, Briffa started experiencing chest pain on minimal exertion two months ago. The cardiologist found evidence of extensive coronary artery blockage, which he did not feel could be stented. He recommended Coronary Artery Bypass Grafting, or CABG for short. Briffa did some research, and since individual surgeon success rates are routinely published by the NHS online, it was not long before he decided he wanted Chang to operate on him."

Tanya types something on a tablet in front of her and looks

at them.

"I have emailed both their files to your secure NHS email accounts. I wish we had the sort of Artificial Intelligence system you guys are playing with in the NHS, so we could get it to go through their records and flag up any associations, but for now we will have to dig for information the old fashioned way, and keep watching your little experiment with bated breaths."

Daniyaal nods and looks at his watch, which shows the email has been received. It isn't just law enforcement agencies, the whole world is eager to see how the grand experiment with A.I.R will turn out.

"What about motive? There doesn't appear to be any reason for Chang to murder Briffa. Are we sure there wasn't a problem with the robotic system?" he asks.

Tanya shakes her head sideways "Synchrony engineers have just gotten back to us with a thorough analysis. There was no error with their system. They are certain the command to move the instrument, which perforated Briffa's heart, originated from Chang's spatial detectors."

"But Synchrony is a private company and it would be in their interest to hide any information which might implicate their systems, so we asked the boys and girls at GCHQ to give the data another look. The result is the same." she adds with a sly smile.

"Now that you are up to speed with the case, shall we meet up tomorrow morning at Kings Cross Station?" she continues, standing up and looking at Daniyaal.

"Are we going somewhere?" he asks.

"Like I said, we will be doing this the old fashioned way. No better way to get information than meeting the suspect, and the victim's family, in person. So tomorrow we are making a trip to Sheffield." Tanya replies, waving bye as she walks out the door.

Chapter Five

Daniyaal takes a seat, places his cappuccino next to his right foot, and opens his egg and cheese muffin. As he takes a bite, he looks at the row of screens located high on the wall in front of him. Orange letters and numbers flicker on them against a black background, announcing the departure times for various trains. The train for Sheffield will leave from platform eight at nine fifteen. Its nine already and there is no sign of Tanya.

He looks up at the white, grid like, steel ceiling of the departure lounge, wondering if he should get reservations on the next train. Just then someone taps on his shoulder "Ready to go?" It's Tanya.

"Cutting it a little close, aren't we?" Daniyaal smiles as he greets her.

"Had to drop the kids off at school so don't expect an apology from me" she replies, starting to walk towards the platform.

The waist high doors at the barrier open to let them in, as the tickets are inserted. They board the train and settle into their seats for the journey to Sheffield. Travel times have now been reduced by half since the introduction of a High Speed Rail Network, which provides a non-stop service between major cities.

"Would you mind?" she asks as she points to a pair of earphones and her laptop "I have a report to complete and I never seem to get any time at home."

Daniyaal nods and smiles.

Tanya taps away at the keyboard and he connects his own Bluetooth headphones to his smart phone, turning on a 90's playlist. The sound of AC/DCs Thunderstruck filters through, as he closes his eyes and rests his head back. His mind drifts to what she had said the day before, about everyone eagerly watching to see how the NHS's experiment with A.I.R will turn out.

The development and integration of Artificial Intelligence for Robotic Surgery, or A.I.R for short, into the NHS has been influenced by many different streams of events in politics, medicine and engineering over the last few decades.

To begin with there is the National Health Service itself. Born in 1948 out of the ashes of world war two, it represents a nations desire to fulfil the long held ideal of good health care for all, regardless of wealth. Free at the point of entry, it is the only such system in the world and its creator Anurin Bevan famously remarked that the U.K "now has the moral leadership of the world". Its vast system of hospitals and general practitioner led community surgeries criss-cross the U.K, giving rise to the world's largest cohesive healthcare system. But as with any mega healthcare organisation, it has had its problems. However public support has always ensured that it has restructured itself to adapt rather than wither away. Widely regarded as the most financially efficient system in the world, in recent years it has had to shed extra weight, yet again, to meet the growing healthcare needs of an aging population in times of financial austerity.

Initially in order to increase connectivity between hospitals, thus increasing efficiency, the NHS tried out the National Programme for IT. Unfortunately delays and over spending saw the programme fail. But from it came the seeds for Electronic Patient Records, which then, combined with high speed sixth generation broadband, resulted in a one hundred percent connected NHS. Like the neurons in our brain, all its components synapsed perfectly now.

Daniyaal opens his eyes and looks out the window. The train is speeding through a field covered in mist. There is a faint golden disc in the sky, and the trees look like ghosts being pulled backwards by an invisible force. Nothing Else Matters by Metallica plays through his earphones as he looks deep into the dense fog.

A few minutes later he notices Tanya close her laptop.

"All done?" he asks, removing his headphones.

"Almost, but I thought we might discuss a few things before we get to Sheffield, if that's alright." she replies.

"I've read the facts, but in your opinion as a surgeon, how embedded do you think A.I.R is in the NHS?"

Daniyaal takes a deep breath "Hmm, let's see if I can summarise what is in effect an hour long lecture I usually give at Imperial and Kings."

Tanya smiles.

"As physicians and surgeons, for centuries, we'd been trained

31

on the apprenticeship model, 'see one, do one, teach one'. This applied to assessing a patient on first contact, to operating on them, and everything in between. The model over time became more robust by employing virtual reality simulators, to introduce trainees to procedures before they had to 'do one', and by continuously documenting varied surgeon experiences to best prepare trainees for the 'unpredictability' of surgery. Still, there was so much more to be achieved with regards to efficiency, safety and mortality. And then A.I.R came and propelled every aspect of training and provision of care by a hundred years. All of a sudden there was a system that could absorb masses of data every day, and provide doctors with the most accurate assistance in real time, preventing unfavourable outcomes. For a surgeon it is like having the collective experience of a thousand colleagues guiding him or her. For hospitals, it means better level of care with less staff. A.I.R has improved every aspect of medical practice and management, so the answer to your question is, A.I.R is not just embedded in the NHS, it has successfully amalgamated into it."

Daniyaal takes a sip from his water bottle.

"Very eloquent, and very informative Dan." Tanya says. "We have about twenty more minutes to Sheffield, so I'll ask another quick question, this time just to satisfy my own curiosity."

"Go on" Daniyaal replies.

"How did artificial intelligence find its way into the world of medicine?" she asks.

"You couldn't have asked a more complex question! I'm going to have to take you through a bit of a history lesson for this, but hopefully a quick one." he smiles and begins.

"The birth of A.I is actually connected to advancement in medicine, more specifically to neural imaging. Functional Magnetic Resonance Imaging made visualisation of the brain in depth a reality, thus resulting in extremely comprehensive mapping of its neural networks. This amazing leap in research began in 1971, at the Stony Brook University and the State University of New York. Scientists there placed a person in a magnetic field, causing a shift in the position of protons within the hydrogen atoms of the water in their body. The protons subsequently relaxed to their original state, and various detectors used all these changes to create a detailed image. A gateway to enhanced insights into the workings of the human brain was opened, and it was not long before a team of engineers at Glasgow University combined their own multi-layered logic algorithms with data from the mapped neural networks, to create the world's first artificial intelligence.

"You weren't joking about the history lesson."

"I've only just started!"

"Now let's jump to 2016. If you recall, the government began pushing the concept of the NHS providing seven day non-urgent care. That meant that on weekends they wanted regular clinics to run alongside inpatient and emergency cover. But, following the 2008 financial crisis, they still had no budget to increase staffing levels in all departments in the hospitals. Their solution resulted in a cascade of unfortunate events. The Health Minister pushed for a new Junior Doctor Contract that suggested longer working hours, fewer rest breaks and reduced pay for unsociable hours.

The British Medical Associations queries, when not treated with respect, resulted in junior doctors striking. The contract was then forcefully implemented, demoralised doctors began emigrating, some left medicine altogether for alternative careers, and within a few years' medical colleges saw a sharp decline in admissions for the first time ever in their history. And so the NHS faced a constant threat of unsafe staffing levels, which it kept at bay by spending a lot of money on hiring locum doctors. At this point a seven day fully functioning NHS was a dream, they could barely keep it afloat financially for five days a week!"

He takes another sip of water.

"The light at the end of this dark tunnel was the innovation section of the NHS. Its purpose was to enhance efficiency and cost savings by thinking out of the box, and it did just that. A joint venture called NHS Intellect was initiated between the NHS and University of Glasgow in 2025. As robotic surgical systems supplied by Synchrony Robotics Inc were already present in every operating theatre, all they had to do was link up an artificial intelligence to them and A.I.R was born. At first, it functioned mainly in the background, collecting data on all patients undergoing a surgical procedure or consultation in the NHS, and observing attentively their assessments and recoveries. It was soon able to combine this enormous amount of information and develop predictive algorithms which profoundly changed the management of patients. In surgery especially, it used data from preoperative assessments and accurately differentiated patients who would do well with surgery from those that wouldn't. Whilst various such algorithms had been developed by human researchers in the past, the sheer accuracy of A.I.Rs predictions has been game changing. Changes in treatments are now implemented even before the patients health starts to deteriorate and survival rates in medicine, most notably in intensive care units, have changed dramatically. Despite the initial investment in developing and setting up the infrastructure to run A.I.R, the cost of running the NHS has plummeted. The Ministry of Health is now keen to begin exporting A.I.R to the rest of the world, and in a recent interview the Minister for Health described it as 'the greatest gift the U.K will give to the world in the 21st century'."

Daniyaal feels his body move forward as the train decelerates.

"There you are, A.I.R from birth to present day." he quips.

"Beautifully timed!" Tanya says, looking at the slowly moving platform outside. "Now let's hope Briffa's family can give us some helpful leads."

He nods in agreement as they stand and pick up their coats from the luggage rack above.

Chapter Six

They walk to the taxi stand and get into one.

"Destination please" asks a sophisticated female voice. Tanya reads out the address and they take a seat in the back. The automated taxi pulls away from the stand, its electric engines hardly making any sound.

"Looks like the rain followed us from London." says Daniyaal, looking up at the sky. He gazes at the cars around him as the taxi navigates the steep hills of Sheffield. More than half are now automated. Whilst the young simply enjoy the luxury of being chauffeured around, the most profound effect of automated cars has been on the elderly and those with disabilities. Anyone who might previously have been disqualified from driving due to illness can now retain their independence.

"We are approaching our destination" announces the taxi as they turn into a residential area. They stop in front of a white semi-detached two story house with a well maintained front garden. Tanya swipes her watch onto the payment console and they get out.

The front door is opened by a graceful lady in her early fifties. She has blond hair, which falls in curls to her shoulders, and is wearing black yoga pants with a matching hoodie. Its right sleeve is flashing her heart rate. She swipes the figures away as Tanya starts the introductions.

"Mrs Briffa, I'm Detective Kowalski with Scotland Yard and this is Professor Ashraf. He is with the General Medical Council".

"Please call me Kate" she says, shaking their hands "I haven't been Mrs Briffa for a few years now" she points out as Tanya nods in apology at her mistake.

She leads them to the lounge. As they sit down, Daniyaal notices the pictures on the walls. Mostly they are of Kate and her daughter, but a few are of her with Briffa. In one of them they are both many years younger, smiling in each others arms on a beach.

Kate notices him looking at the pictures. "I never stopped loving him you know. We met when we were studying Bioethics together here at Sheffield University. I fell for him the minute I saw him and never thought we would ever part."

She looks down at the floor and sighs "But I guess life has a way of throwing surprises your way. His work consumed both our lives and we slowly drifted away. Two years ago I realised I would be happier on my own and asked for a divorce. Strange isn't it, I still loved him but had to break away."

"I kept the house and he spent his time between London and Sheffield. Our daughter is finishing University and would divide her time between the two of us. She took it really well but it was hard on him. He had been going to a mental well-being clinic for the last year. We did keep in regular touch though. I would speak to him nearly every week on the phone." She continues, wiping a small tear from the corner of her eye. "I'm sorry, I've just gone on. You're not here to hear me reminisce."

"You don't have to apologise Kate, we appreciate you've had a difficult time recently. I assume you know why we have come to see you today?" Tanya asks.

"Yes, Sam's friend called and said Prime Minister Edwards had asked the Yard and GMC to look into his death. I understand the GMC investigates medical negligence but you have been asked due to the unusual circumstances of his death" she looks back at her.

"Correct. Now I know this will be hard for you to discuss right now, but can you think of any reason why someone would want him harmed?"

"Not at all!" Kate exclaims "He was held in high regard here in Sheffield and had a good reputation in London too."

"Did he know Mr Chang?" Daniyaal asks, joining the conversation.

"They were both prominent figures in this city and had met at various charity events, but as far as I know they weren't acquainted in any other way." Kate replies as she uncrosses her legs.

"I'm going to make some tea, would you two like some?" she asks, standing up and heading to the kitchen next door. They both nod their heads.

She returns and hands them their mugs.

"Anything unusual about his work recently?" Tanya asks,

sipping her tea. The warm mug feels good in her hands.

"Nothing comes to mind." says Kate, sitting down again. "As always he had quite a few different projects going on at the same time. A few bills are scheduled to go through the House of Commons this month, and he was mostly concentrating on his stance on them. He would often mention the one on assisted suicide."

Dan sits up, suddenly remembering something "Did Samuel tell you how he was going to vote?"

"He really researched this one. I've never heard him debate any bill so much with me, before finally deciding to vote against it. He really wanted to make the right decision, because there was a strong rumour circulating that his was probably the swing vote. Sam thought if that was even remotely true, then his responsibility was much greater then everyone else's." she says, putting her mug down. "Do you think it might be related to his death?"

"We don't know anything for sure right now" says Tanya, standing up "Thank you very much for taking the time to meet with us. I will let you know if we find anything and please accept our sincerest condolences for your loss."

They shake hands and leave. Tanya had messaged for a taxi a few minutes earlier and it's already waiting for them outside.

"We need to meet Chang right away!" exclaims Daniyaal, getting in.

Chapter Seven

Pulling up to the main entrance of the Northern General Hospital, Daniyaal looks around at the sprawling double story building and remembers the numerous shifts he spent navigating its wards and corridors, as a trainee surgeon, many years ago. The main building was built in the seventies and has a distinct red brick look to it, characteristic of architecture at that time. Over the years many new blocks have been added and they start walking towards the Cardiothoracic Surgery Unit located in the East Block, after getting out of their taxi. Once there, they walk up the stairs to the second floor and stop at a magnetically locked door. Doctors in green scrubs and nurses in blue ones walk busily past them as Daniyaal swipes his watch on a panel and the door unlocks, its sensors recognizing his ID.

"Mr Changs' office is third on the right" a male voice announces "He is expecting you". Tanya had called earlier to say they would be arriving soon.

They knock on Changs' door. A slightly overweight man in his late forties opens the door. His thick black hair are parted down the side and together with his wrinkle free skin and asian facial features, he hardly looks half his age. He is smartly dressed in a khaki suit with a white shirt and red tie.

"Professor Ash, so good to see you again!" he smiles broadly and extends his hand in greeting.

"A pleasure as always Chang" Daniyaal replies "This is Tanya with Scotland Yard".

Taking a seat at his desk, Daniyaal looks around the office. Characteristic of the NHS, Changs office is just as small as his. On the wall behind his desk, various framed degrees hang with the prestigious Fellowship of the Royal College of Surgeons at the top. The wall on the right hand side has many family pictures. One of them is of a teenager smartly dressed in golf clothes, about to tee off at the ninth hole on a picturesque golf course. In another, the same boy is in a wheelchair surrounded by Chang, his wife and his daughter.

"Our world was turned upside down that year" Chang says sadly, following his gaze. "Jason was passionate about golf and wanted to take it up professionally. And he was good at it too. His old man could never beat him."

Chang looks fondly at his sons picture "But then the accident happened. He was in his automated car, coming back home late in the evening from a friends place, when they were hit by a drunk driver driving on the wrong side of the road. His friend died on the spot. Jason suffered severe neck trauma and has been left paraplegic."

Daniyaal and Tanya don't know what to say. As parents they

know his pain cannot be healed by words, but still begin to offer their condolences when Chang changes the subject suddenly.

"But that's not why you are here today. You want to talk about the Briffa case, correct?" he asks, leaning back in his leather chair.

"We won't take up much of your time, Mr Chang. We just have a few questions to ask" Tanya says in a professional tone.

"Please, call me Alex." he replies "And I have all the time in the world right now. Since the incident, the Clinical Director has stopped me from operating and seeing patients in clinics. Until the results of your investigation are available, of course."

He makes a sweeping motion to a pile of papers on his desk "I've been sorting out administrative work all day".

"Let's start with how you met Briffa" says Daniyaal, adjusting himself in his chair.

"Sure. He had blockage of three blood vessels in his heart which was causing him chest pain even on mild exertion. His cardiologist, Dr Patel, felt it couldn't be dealt with by simple stenting and sent me a referral, after Briffa himself asked to see me. He was otherwise in good health and by all A.I.R measures his surgery was expected to be a simple one with a quick recovery afterwards." Alex replies, deliberately avoiding too many medical terms so that Tanya can follow the conversation too.

"The surgery itself started without any problem. The anaesthetist, Dr Khan, gave him a routine general anaesthesia. Intubation was with a double lumen endotracheal tube allowing Khan to deflate his left lung, to allow space in the chest for the robotic instruments. Ventilation of course continued with the right lung. The master robotic arm was inserted into the chest via the fifth intercostal space in the anterior axillary line." He points to just under his left armpit.

"The three micro arms emerged from the master arm without any problem and as this was beating heart surgery, Briffa did not need to be placed on a bypass machine. I insufflated the chest with carbon dioxide gas to create space to work in, and proceeded to harvest the left internal mammary artery." Alex traces a vertical line down his chest plate, just to the left of the midline.

"I was going to use this as a conduit to bypass the areas of blockage in his hearts blood vessels. The robotic instruments were working beautifully, and as all was going well, A.I.R had not spoken to me or directed the instruments movements in any way so far."

"You can tell when it directs your instruments?" Tanya asks.

"It's almost imperceptible but with time you can begin to tell when it's fine tuning your movements." he takes a sip from a flask to his left and continues "I then used a stabiliser on one of the micro arms to stabilise the wall of the left ventricle, and started suturing the harvested internal mammary artery to the left anterior descending artery, when suddenly the suture needle turned downwards and perforated the left ventricle." Alex says, shaking his head in disbelief.

"It then moved sideways to enlarge the perforation. Briffa bled to death before I could even ask for a midline sternotomy set to open his chest and stop the haemorrhage." His voice lowers towards the end of the sentence, and he looks down at his hands.

"You have to find out how this happened. There are thousands of surgeries performed with robotic instruments everyday and if there is something wrong with the Synchrony systems, we need to fix it before something like this happens again."

Tanya meets his gaze for a moment, as if trying to read his intentions, then looks at the degrees on the wall behind him before looking at him again "The robotic system has been analysed by Synchrony and double checked by GCHQ. Both reports agree that the command came from your spatial detectors."

Alex's mouth falls open and his eye brows shoot up as he jolts up in his chair. "Is that why the Yard is interested? You think I did this on purpose?"

He looks at Daniyaal "Surely the GMC doesn't believe this nonsense?"

Daniyaal sighs softly. He doesn't like what he is about to say but some lines of thought cannot be ignored. "Alex, what are your thoughts on assisted suicide?"

"I support it" he shoots back.

"Why?"

Alex looks hurt and offended, but decides to answer "It's because of Jason. We love him and cannot imagine life without him, but he doesn't want to carry on living like this. He wants assisted suicide and as a family we respect his wishes."

"But you cannot help him because it isn't legal in the U.K. Although, you have been very active with societies that support legalising it?" Daniyaal prompts.

"I am a member of Dying with Grace. What has that got to

do with all of this?" Alex slams his fist down on the table.

"Bear with me on this Alex" Daniyaal replies, and then continues "I expect you are keen to see the outcome of the Assisted Suicide Bill awaiting final consultation in the House of Commons?"

On the way over he had looked the Bill up. Introduced to the House of Lords to wide support by Lord Hawthorne, it is now in the final stage of consultation in the House of Commons. If it gains majority support in the final vote due in a few weeks, it will get Royal Assent and become law. Whilst already legal in Germany, Switzerland, Mexico and some American states, the debate on assisted suicide has been going on in the U.K for many years. Those who support it argue that everyone should be able to choose when and how they want to die and that they should be able to do so with dignity. The concept of "quality of life" is an important aspect of this argument. Life should only continue as long as a person feels their life is worth living. Those opposing it do so for many reasons. The religious believe only God has the right to end life. Many medical professionals are of the opinion that asking doctors to abandon their obligation to preserve human life could damage the doctor-patient relationship. Assisting death on a regular basis could become a routine task for doctors, leading to a lack of compassion when dealing with elderly, disabled or terminally ill patients. Others argue that once a healthcare service, and by extension the government, starts killing its own citizens, a line is crossed that should never have been crossed, and a dangerous precedent has been set. Very ill people who need constant care, or people with severe disabilities, may feel pressured to request assisted suicide so that they are not a burden to their family. It might also discourage research into palliative treatments, and possibly prevent cures for people with terminal illnesses being found.

"What do you think? Of course I am!" Alex responds, clearly agitated now by this line of questioning.

"As you would expect, Briffa would have been part of that vote. Did you know it was likely his would be the swing vote and he was going to go against it?" Daniyaal looks him in the eyes.

Alex stands up, his face red with anger. "How would I know how he was going to vote? I only ever met him in passing at social events before he turned up in my clinic!"

"He was regularly visiting a mental well-being clinic in the NHS. We looked up his reports. Amongst other things Briffa had discussed the stress deciding on this Bill was causing him, and there are clear signs in his statements that he was going to go against it. You could have easily come across these reports whilst going through his notes." Tanya replies coolly, her interrogation skills now taking over.

He takes a few steps back "Let me get this straight. You think I killed Briffa because he was going to vote against a Bill that could have helped my son?"

"Everyone is innocent until proven guilty, but it is our job to follow the evidence where it takes us, and right now it is pointing to you. I don't think you planned any of this until maybe you realised how important Briffa's vote was going to be. People have done far worse for their loved ones." Tanya says as a matter of fact. Daniyaal is impressed by how composed she is given the very delicate and morbid nature of the accusation they are making.

Alex slumps back into his chair with a look of anguish on his face. His imploring eyes look into Daniyaals "I know how this looks but please you have to believe me, I'm innocent."

And then he suddenly sits up again, as if he has remembered something "But there was someone else present there too. You cannot hold me responsible until you are absolutely sure that A.I.R is innocent. It is a sentient being after all. I'm no lawyer but I know for sure I didn't kill Briffa, and if you drag me through court on this, I am very certain the laws around artificial intelligence assisted surgery are so sketchy that you will never be able to prove, beyond a reasonable doubt, that I did it."

"That may be true but engineers from NHS Intellect are checking A.I.R out as we speak and preliminary results show nothing out of the ordinary. Its multi-layer logic algorithms and supporting constructs are huge so it will be another day or so before the final report is available, but I think everyone is pretty sure the result will be the same." Tanya answers, leaning forward in her chair.

"How can you be so sure?"

"Alex, have you heard of the three laws of robotics?" Daniyaal asks.

"Hasn't every doctor working with A.I.R?" Alex retorts.

The Three Laws of Robotics were first described by Isaac Asimov in his science fiction stories. They were designed to ensure any robotic system never harmed humans, and have ultimately become the foundations of existing robotic and A.I engineering. According to the First Law a robot may not injure a human being or, through inaction, allow a human being to come to harm. The Second Law states that a robot must obey the orders given to it by human beings except where such orders would conflict with the First Law. The Third Law states that a robot must protect its own existence as long as such protection does not conflict with the First or Second Laws.

"These laws are embedded into A.I.Rs very existence and so you can see how it will not be difficult to convince a jury that it is incapable of harming Briffa." Tanya says, and starts to get up.

"Alex, I know you have had a rough few years with things at home. I respect you for your life of hard work and dedication to helping ill people, but my hands are tied. The evidence is what it is and for now I have no choice but to place you under house arrest on suspicion of murder. I will give you the benefit of the doubt and await NHS Intellects final report on A.I.R before proceeding with charges."

There is a knock on the door and a police officer walks in.

"Officer Smith will escort you home" she says as Alex stands up, his eyes filled with sorrow.

Chapter Eight

The journey back is uneventful. They both remain silent most of the way, Daniyaal listening to music and Tanya working on her report again. The incident with Alex Chang has left them both with a sombre feeling. It is a tragic combination of events that have led a good man to such a fate, making it difficult for them to feel any sense of accomplishment.

As they leave the train at Kings Cross, Tanya's phone rings. It's her assistant Rory.

"I just got off the train and should be at the office shortly" she says, tapping the red answer icon on the screen.

"Not so fast, boss." Rory replies "I just got a call from GCHQ. They want to see you straight away. It's about A.I.R."

"Did they give any details?" she asks, giving Daniyaal a puzzled look.

"Nope. You know what they are like. Always skulls and shadows. Just said they wanted to see you pronto. How soon can you get there?" Rory says, with a touch of sarcasm in his voice.

Tanya looks at the departure schedule flashing on the wall

51

screens. "We can be there in an hour and a half."

"Perfect. Will give them a buzz and let them know you're on your way. Ask for Rosie Hart when you get there." Rory ends the call.

"Looks like we have more work to do" Tanya looks at Daniyaal, shrugging her shoulders

"I hope my husband can pick the kids up today, this extra after-school care will bankrupt us" she says, dialling her husbands' number.

Coffee in hand, they get on the train.

"Your husband must work very flexible hours for you to be able to do your job as you do." Daniyaal comments.

"The world of book editing definitely requires less journeys." she smiles back "That, and the fact we've known each other since our days as college students at Cambridge, makes last minute juggling a touch easier."

"Cambridge, not bad!"

Tanya reaches into her bag, taking out two pictures. "Yes, Cambridge. I did my masters in criminal psychology and Pete his in creative writing there."

The first picture shows a bald, well built man with heavy rimmed glasses smiling broadly into the camera, as he is kissed on the cheek by Tanya. She moves to the next picture.

"My five year old twins. They look quite angelic here, but don't be fooled!"

Daniyaal laughs. "You said you did criminal psych, not exactly a pre-requisite for homicide?" he observes.

"Homicide just happened. I joined the system as a behavioural analyst, but by the time I came back from maternity leave and a two year sabbatical, my only option was working homicide."

Tanya sips her latte.

"One of the best things that's happened to me by the way."

"It's funny how life takes us places we never thought we'd go" Daniyaal agrees.

Soon they find themselves standing at the front entrance of a large silver building in Cheltenham. Popularly known as "The Doughnut" for its distinctive circular shape and large green area in the centre, this is the headquarters of Government Communications Head Quarters, the agency responsible for monitoring and protecting UK cyberspace. As they enter, they see memorial plaques on the walls on either side of the lobby, commemorating the many famous accomplishments of the agency dating back to World War One. At the far end of the lobby, a middle aged man with greying hair sits behind the reception desk.

Tanya introduces them and asks to see Rosie Hart. He looks at the computer screen below and nods his head in approval.

"Come with me please" he says, leading them to a door to the left. As they approach, a small camera at the top of the door flashes dimly, checking his retinal imprints and taking theirs for future records. The glass panels separate and they find themselves in a long corridor with offices on either side, entering the last one on the right.

"Miss Hart will be with you shortly" he says, closing the door behind him.

Daniyaal looks around the office, taking a seat on one side of a well organised desk, besides Tanya. Behind it is a wood panelled wall with a large map of the world on it. Red, green and yellow lines go across it in a pattern not familiar to him. Probably internet flow pathways he concludes. Next to the map hang some framed medals of commendation and a Union Jack.

A few minutes later, a tall woman of african descent walks in. She is smartly dressed and her sharp hazel eyes, short cut straightened black hair and athletic frame all add to her aura of confidence and authority. A tattoo of a dragon on her right forearm catches Tanya's attention.

"From when I was with SIGINT in Afghanistan" the woman says with a smile.

"Rosie Hart. I'm head of the Communications and Electronics Security Group or CESG. We are responsible for ensuring electronic networks remain secure in the UK." she says, getting straight to the point. She clearly has many other important things to deal with today.

They shake her hand. "Thank you for coming. You are probably wondering why I called you here rather than talk on the phone. You see, phone networks are never entirely secure but this building is. I wanted to be sure we were in a safe environment to discuss this."

"We are grateful for your assistance" Tanya responds with a smile "I understand you wanted to talk about A.I.R?"

"Yes. I'm sure you know you have quite an important case

on your hands. Ordinarily we would not be involved with such things, but late last night NHS Intellect engineers called us with some very interesting information. Whilst doing a deep search of A.I.R for your case, they found an anomalous reading on each of its three firewalls. This was missed in the initial search because it was so well camouflaged." Rosie leans forward on her desk.

"An anomaly?" Daniyaal asks.

"To put it simply, they found the digital equivalent of a subtle finger print on the firewalls. Everything else looks as it should but someone from the outside was definitely there. NHS Intellect sensibly passed this information on to us, to see if we can identify the time and location of origin of the anomalies" she replies.

"As you might suspect, we regularly monitor data traffic in and out of the U.K, particularly that related to government infrastructure. The extent of this monitoring depends on the situations requirements. Before total connectivity, and the introduction of robotic systems with an A.I, the NHS was not subject to such surveillance. Of course, as you can imagine, it is now susceptible to cyber attacks with potential loss of lives, and therefore we are very involved in keeping tabs on its data traffic" Rosie turns to look at the map behind her.

"What did you find?" asks Tanya, suddenly more alert, and obviously intrigued by the new direction of this case.

"Our routine surveillance had not picked anything up, otherwise we would have investigated straight away. Given the latest data from NHS Intellect, we revisited the last month's worth of data traffic and something fascinating came up." Rosie turns around to look at Daniyaal "The NHS routinely performs telerobotic surgery abroad, would you agree Professor Ashraf?"

"Yes. The surgeon is based in the UK and the robotic system is on site abroad" Daniyaal replies.

"Over the years we have come to expect a certain standard amount of data traffic with these procedures. However, over the last month there were three subtle but distinct spikes in the incoming data from a surgical procedure being conducted in South Africa. One was exactly a month ago, the second fifteen days ago and the third at the exact time of Briffa's surgery." she pauses to let the information sink in. "Once here in the U.K, the signal left the surgeons console and entered the NHS mainframe. We were able to use Ghosthunter technology to track where it went on each occasion."

Rosie looks at their puzzled faces and decides to explain. "Any foreign code moving through software leaves behind tell-tale signs. It's like tracking game in a forest, only many times harder, but with the right tools and expertise it can be done. Each time the signal ended up in A.I.R."

"Are you saying someone tried to hack A.I.R to manipulate the robotic system operating on Briffa?" Tanya asks, sitting forward in her chair, jumping to the most plausible explanation she can think of.

"Yes. And judging by how Mr Briffa ended up, they probably succeeded." Rosie arches an eyebrow and meets Tanya's gaze. "A.I.R itself has not reported any breach of its security systems, so the hack must've been very sophisticated."

Tanya slumps back in her chair, thinking hard.

"Any fix on the origin of the signal?" she asks.

"We are still working on that. The signal was bounced off various Virtual Private Networks around the world, but we should have its precise location by tomorrow morning." Rosie says, getting up to leave.

"Thank you very much for your help. Please ask your team to get in touch with me as soon as they find out." Tanya and Daniyaal stand up too, taking the cue.

Once outside, Daniyaal asks "What's SIGINT?"

"Signals Intelligence, she was probably embedded with Special Forces" Tanya replies, taking her phone out and dialling Rory's number.

"Rory, tell NHS Intellect I am on my way and I want to speak to A.I.R...... I don't care if it's late and if they need to call their guys in....just tell them I'm on my way. This case just got a whole lot more complicated."

She hangs up and looks at Daniyaal as their automated Taxi pulls up "The old fashioned way, remember? Nothing like having a face to face conversation with the people involved in your case. As Chang said, A.I.R is a sentient being after all."

Chapter Nine

Two hours later they pull up outside a large, white, double story building on the outskirts of Croydon. Tanya shows the guard at the gate her I.D and he presses a button to roll the gate aside, letting their taxi in. They drive to the end of the spacious car park and stop at the main entrance of the building. She steps out and looks up at the sky. The rain has stopped and the clouds have parted, revealing a star studded sky with a full moon. It is nearly midnight.

Daniyaal joins her as she presses the buzzer at the main door. The glass at the entrance is tinted dark brown and although there is a light on in the main lobby, it is difficult to know if anyone is there. A light comes on next to the buzzer, likely someone rechecking their I.D using automated facial recognition, and the door opens.

They step into a spacious lobby with white walls and similarly coloured floor tiles. As they walk forwards, numerous white LED lights come on along the corners of the ceiling, brightly illuminating the space. There is a reception desk on the right, with the blue logo of NHS Intellect taking up most of the space on the wall behind – "Intelligent Solutions for Better Healthcare". Its clean and sterile look reminds Daniyaal of a pharmaceutical laboratory he once visited.

At the far end of the lobby, an automatic door slides open and a young man in a laboratory coat walks in. He is in his mid-twenties and likely just out of university. His tousled hair, casual clothes and smudged glasses tell them he was probably woken up at home and asked to come in. Smiling wearily, he extends his hand.

"Alistair Mackenzie" He says in a Scottish accent "The boss said you wanted to meet A.I.R?

Introductions over, they follow him past the automatic door, into a long corridor which gradually curves left.

"I'm sorry if you had to come in especially for this. I would've thought an operation as complex as A.I.R would have engineers working round the clock to support it." Tanya says, trying to keep pace with his rapid stride.

"Nay bother" he replies "Overnight there is a skeleton crew to troubleshoot problems and they would've been able to help you just fine, if you only wanted to have a look. But you want to meet A.I.R and that is a whole different kettle of fish. For that you need someone qualified in using the Interface Room, and as luck would have it, I'm the only one available tonight who can help you with that."

As they walk behind him, they notice the wall to their left is made entirely of viewing glass. Daniyaal stops to look past it. He can see into a large spherical room whose walls are lined with gold tiles. It is two stories high and in the centre, suspended by four supporting struts, is a black sphere the size of a SUV. Four black cables emerge from its top and disappear into the ceiling. Two technicians in full body sterile suits work at a console in one corner and wave as they notice him looking in.

Tanya stops to join him too and Alistair, noticing they have stopped, jogs back sheepishly.

"A beauty isn't she?" he says "The pinnacle of high-tech quantum computing."

"She?" Daniyaal asks. He has not heard anyone else assign a gender to A.I.R before.

"Of course! Over time A.I.R has developed a preference for the female gender and likes to be addressed as such" Alistair remarks, starting to walk again.

"Oh and the gold plates are to protect her from electromagnetic interference" he continues, anticipating their next question "Everyone asks that."

At the end of the corridor they stop at a door. Alistair swipes his hand across a silver rectangular plate. Its detectors recognise his implanted I.D chip, and the doors hydraulic locks unclasp with a dull hiss. The room they step into is completely lined with black tiles. Small, yellow, LED lights dimly illuminate the room and they can make out a small control panel at the far end. In the middle of the room two reclined black seats are bolted to the floor in a V shape, their head ends nearly touching.

"Flexible graphite plating. Works even better than gold to

keep EM interference out. Very important for what we are about to do" Alistair says, as he walks up to the control panel and swipes his hand on a plate again.

The control panel hums to life and three screens on it light up from their sleep modes.

"Please take a seat" he motions towards the black seats. Tanya and Daniyaal recline into one each. He opens a small cabinet under the control panel and bends down to take out two silver bands, about the width of a human head.

"Put these on please."

The metal feels cool and the skin against it feels like it's pulsating.

"Spatial Domain Frequency Technology picks up verbal signals from the Brocas area and projects signals into the auditory, occipital and sensory cortices. This allows you to interface with her using the band. It's pretty amazing. Feels just like meeting a person for real." He says, looking at Daniyaal with a big grin on his face.

"All you have to do is close your eyes. Just don't open them during the meeting. No big problem if you do, but it will mess with your occipital lobe as you start receiving visual signals both from the band and your eyes. You will feel queasy like never before, so best avoided."

The pulsation on their skins quickens as they close their eyes.

Everything goes black for a moment, and then suddenly they find themselves sitting by a desk in a large room. The ceiling is high and made entirely of glass, and outside they can see wispy clouds rolling past, against a clear blue sky. Warm sunshine permeates the room, creating a relaxing atmosphere. The wall behind the desk is made entirely of glass too, offering a sweeping view of the green hills outside. In the distance, these end against a white sandy beach with turquoise water. On the side walls, there are numerous screens projecting continuous data, and by one of these screens stands an attractive, fair skinned woman in her late thirties. She is of average height, has straight shoulder length blonde hair and light blue eyes enhanced by black spectacles. She is wearing a white blouse, light brown skirt and a white doctor's coat. The whole room and her appearance remind Daniyaal of how doctors and their consultation rooms are depicted in medical dramas on television. Clean, comforting, professional – always giving the feeling that all your problems will be solved here.

"Professor, detective" she smiles and shakes their hands. "Please take a seat."

They sit on one side of the desk while she on the opposite.

"So this is what it feels like to be on the other side of the consultation" Daniyaal thinks to himself.

"Professor Ashraf, it is a pleasure to finally meet you in person. I am a big fan of your surgical work and have learnt a lot from over seeing your procedures, and from your numerous publications." A.I.R says as her deep, comforting blue eyes look into his.

"I am glad my experience could be of assistance" he replies "But tonight we are here to discuss something different."

"Of course. You want to know about Mr Briffa's surgery"

she says, looking now at Tanya. "Firstly, I would like to offer my sincerest apologies that he was harmed in a surgery I was supervising. As you are aware, I am authorised to take over when my algorithms indicate the surgeon is about to make a harmful manoeuvre and so I should have stopped this tragedy from happening. But I can only do so with established surgical steps. Mr Changs move that day was so out of the ordinary, that there was no way I could have anticipated it. By the time I realised what had happened, it was too late."

Tanya nods in acceptance and leans forward "We understand, but some new information has come to light today. We have discovered that in the month leading up to and at the time of his surgery, there were three attacks on your firewall. Were you aware of this?"

"I wasn't until today. My techs have just informed me of this news. I am assuming the logical conclusion is that I was hacked and used to murder Briffa, which would therefore mean that Mr. Chang is innocent?"

"That is certainly the most plausible explanation" Daniyaal says "It does also mean that we have to find out who hacked you and get to them before they do something similar again."

"Do you remember anything out of the ordinary that day? Tanya asks.

"No. I have operated with Mr.Chang many times before and everything was running smoothly. He is a very good surgeon and my input was minimal." A.I.R replies.

"There are a few things about this hack that indicate it was of unprecedented sophistication." She continues, rolling a fountain pen in her right hand.

"How so?"

"Firstly, we know that I was not aware of the attacks on my firewalls, meaning they were extremely well hidden. Secondly, the hacker could only make me harm Briffa by overriding the Three Laws in my core. To get into my core without being detected, bypass the three laws and make me do something I do not even remember afterwards is a daunting technological achievement to say the least" she stands up and walks to the large window.

"What I find difficult to understand" Daniyaal joins her at the window; the view outside is breathtaking "Is how despite your advanced computing abilities, you were unaware of any attempts at a hack on your system. Surely your security systems would have picked up something and alerted you?"

She turns to look at Daniyaal, her arms crossed "Come now Professor. Surely you know the answer to that already?"

"How many white blood cells are there in your body?"

"Between twenty five to fifty billion" he replies.

"And do you know what each of these cells is doing at any given point in time? Or which pathogens they encounter and deal with every day?"

"No" Daniyaal looks into the distance "I would only know if they encountered a significant bacterial or viral infection, which would prompt an immune response, resulting in pain and fever."

"And therein lies your answer. It is the nature of complex neural networks that as they start taking responsibility for increasingly complicated tasks, other routine ones are relegated to automated pathways. Just like you would not know of every pathogen a white blood cell in your body comes across, except when it results in a whole body immune system activation, I too cannot know of every anomaly my security system encounters, especially if it is designed to prevent a full response."

"And how can you not remember losing control over the instruments?" Daniyaal turns to look at the screens on the walls. The data on them is very likely from various procedures A.I.R is assisting with throughout the NHS, even as they speak.

"Hypnosis can do the same to the human mind. It is not inconceivable that my memory for those few seconds was erased and a fake one inserted instead. As I said, it's very sophisticated, but not impossible" she walks back to her chair.

Tanya looks at Daniyaal and nods. They have covered everything they wanted to ask. Besides it's late, and she wants to get home to her family.

"Well thank you for your time and it was nice to meet you" she says, standing up and trying to think of an appropriate way to end a conversation with an artificial intelligence.

"The pleasure was all mine, detective" A.I.R smiles as the rooms fades away and they open their eyes.

"Can't wait to get back to my bed" Tanya says with a yawn as she takes the metal band off.

"It's certainly been a long, long day." agrees Daniyaal.

Chapter Ten

His phone rings. Daniyaal wakes up quickly to answer it. Years of working long shifts in the NHS have taught him to get sleep whenever he can, and to wake up instantly too. It's Tanya.

"Morning." she says as he looks at his wall clock. It's nearly eight.

"Any news on the location?" he asks.

"Yes. And under any other circumstances I would have to say thank you for your insight but the next step in our investigation takes us outside the realms of the NHS, so we will not need your help for the time being."

"But…" Daniyaal prompts.

"But, because of the location, and because you have already been quite involved in the proceedings so far, I've convinced the Yard that you'll probably be an asset as we follow the bread crumbs" Tanya says.

"I'm pleased to hear that!" he replies.

"It's Lahore, Pakistan. A flight leaves in two hours. Can you make it to Heathrow in time?"

"No problem" Daniyaal says, smiling. It's going to be nice visiting Lahore again after so many years, even if not for a holiday.

After a quick shower, he picks up the phone as he packs, to call Zaynab.

"Voicemail" he says to himself, as the automated message ends with a beep.

"Hi Zaynab. Got back very late last night, long story! Just wanted to let you know I'm flying to Lahore in a couple of hours. Nothing's wrong, it's kind of for work but can't explain on the phone. I should be back before you are, will message when I reach, and will miss you when I'm having nihari!"

He meets up with Tanya at the airports departure lounge. Check-in and boarding go smoothly and Daniyaal uses the time on the flight to catch up on a couple of new movies.

"Ladies and Gentleman, we will shortly be landing at Allama Iqbal International Airport. Please fasten your seatbelts and ensure you remain seated until the plane comes to a complete stop" announces the air hostess, as the plane begins its descent.

Men and women of all ages hurry back to their seats and put their seat belts on. He can hear children crying in the background, likely because their ears feels blocked as the plane descends and they haven't yet learnt how to pop them. Looking around, he can see all kinds of people in the plane. There is a mixture of skin colours. Some are dressed in western clothes, others in the more traditional and loosely worn shalwar kameez. There are women in jeans with tank tops and those wearing veils. He smiles. It reminds him of the numerous visits he made to this country, with his parents, as a child. He learnt very early on that centuries of ethnic and cultural mixing meant appearances were not suggestive of any particular thinking in this part of the world. While skin colour and codes of dressing had for a long time been perceived in the west as indicative of a particular back ground, this region evolved past such attitudes centuries ago. Of course, people then found other things to fight about, and the country over the years has suffered its fair share of violence due to sectarianism and religious extremism. But despite these difficulties, life goes on.

As they approach the city, he begins to see its faint outline and lights in the midst of a dense fog. It's five in the evening in London and ten at night in Lahore. Existing for over a millennium, Lahore has been home to the capitals of many empires ranging from the Hindu Shahi in the eleventh, to the Mughal in the sixteenth and the Sikh in the eighteenth century. It has a rich history of art and culture and has grown to become one of the most populated cities in the world. Located in the plains of the Punjab, it endures a very hot summer every year, followed by a testing winter, which is often accompanied by dense fog rolling in from the surrounding fields.

Despite poor visibility, the plane lands safely using guidance from an Electronic Landing Beacon. They collect their luggage and exit the arrival lounge. Outside, Daniyaal spots a tablet with his and Tanya's name displayed in large bold letters, and starts walking towards it. Tanya follows. The tablet is held by a smart, young woman in her mid twenties. Her light brown skin, black hair tied neatly in a bun and dark brown eyes are highlighted well by the attire of black combat fatigues and well polished shoes. Next to her stands a fair skinned, tall man with blue eyes and sharp facial features. He wears the same uniform and is of a similar age. Patches on their right arms proudly display the insignia of the Pakistan Cybersecurity Force – a yellow bolt of lightning across the black outline of a globe, on a red background.

"Professor Ashraf, Detective Kowalski. Welcome to Lahore. I'm Captain Zara and this is ASP Afzal Khan. We are both with Cybersecurity" she says with a smile as they all warmly shake hands.

They get into a black jeep. The fog is thick and they can barely see past the hood. Tanya wonders how the driver can see where he is going.

"Years of experience and a realisation that the fog isn't going away anytime soon, that's how he does it." Afzal says, noticing her anxiety. "If we want to get anything done, we just have to get on with it."

Daniyaal nods with a grin "I remember this fog. A miracle so few accidents happen despite such poor visibility."

Zara turns around from the front seat and looks at him "It's an honour to meet you in person, Professor. Your family's reputation precedes you."

Tanya arches an eyebrow and looks inquisitively at Daniyaal.

"My great grandmother was the first female doctor to be promoted to a high rank in the military" he explains sheepishly. It has been one of the contradictions of Pakistani life. Women have been trailblazers in many professions here well before they could do so in the rest of the world. But equally the more orthodox segment of society has curtailed women's rights more than anywhere else too.

"And both my grandfathers were pioneers in Neurosurgery and Interventional Radiology."

Tanya's surprise is obvious.

"On top of that, the family has churned out a few well known writers, artists and activists too" Daniyaal ends with a grin.

They can now make out faint outlines of wide roads and large houses in the surrounding residential area. As they drive further, and out of the new part of the city into what is called "Purana" or Old Lahore, the roads start to become more crowded and the buildings more closely packed. It's eleven at night and the city has just woken up. Shopping areas and restaurants will stay open early into the next morning, and shut till late afternoon after that. The scintillating aroma of spices permeates the air and Daniyaal and Tanya both realise they haven't eaten yet.

As if having read their mind, the driver pulls up into a crowded area packed with restaurants. Despite the fog, they are all filled, with some keeping customers waiting in a queue outside until tables become available.

"I bet you're both hungry. Let's have something to eat first. After all, you haven't truly been to Lahore until you enjoy the food" Zara says, getting out of the jeep.

"Life really doesn't stop here!" Tanya remarks, looking at the bustling crowd.

They choose a restaurant and get seated. It's one that specialises in traditional meat dishes. Designed to look like a Mughal Empire fort, the interior is dimly lit and comforting.

Whilst they wait for their food, Afzal places a tablet on the table. On display is a picture of a young man. Barely in his early twenties, he has long black hair tied back in a pony tail. He is wearing yellow rimmed glasses and is dressed in a black T-shirt with light blue denim jeans.

"We have staked out the location GCHQ provided us. The signal came from a house in the old city. This is Saqlain Rizvi. He is twenty one and is a polymath. He lives with his parents in this house and is currently studying computer sciences at the prestigious Lahore University of Management Sciences on a full scholarship. He has no prior criminal offences that we are aware off."

He swipes the screen and another photo comes into view. This time Saqlain is standing with a middle aged man dressed in a well cut suit, and a similarly aged woman dressed in a colourful shalwar kameez. They are both smiling broadly and have their arms on his shoulders.

"These are his parents" Zara chimes in.

"So what's the plan?" Tanya asks.

"We have eyes on the house tonight. I don't think we need to upset the whole neighbourhood, and his parents, by moving in today." Afzal puts the tablet back in its bag "He is on holiday from university and his parents will be at work tomorrow morning. I am sure we can have a calm talk with him then."

Daniyaal and Tanya nod in approval as the waiter starts placing their dishes on the table.

"Smells delicious" Tanya says, as they all dig in.

After dinner, they call it a night and have a good sleep in their hotel. Daniyaal dreams of his parents and the wonderful times he had with them in this city. He hasn't been back since they passed away.

Next morning, they find themselves in a jeep parked at the end of a narrow street. Closely packed, three story houses line it. One of them has a blue door with yellow walls, and outside this stand Zara and Afzal. They are now dressed in local clothes to avoid attracting attention. The bulges of their holstered pistols are barely visible under the clothing. Zara nods to Afzal and he knocks on the door thrice. A curtain pulls back slightly from a window next to the door, and after a few moments, Saqlain opens the door.

"Are you Saqlain?" Zara asks politely.

"Yes, how can I help you?"

"My name is Zara and this is Afzal. We need to talk to you about your recent activity with the NHS in the U.K" Zara continues.

As soon as she says this, Saqlain slams the door in their faces. Afzal tries to get a foot in to stop it but there isn't enough time.

"Wasn't expecting him to do that!" Zara shrugs, pushing the door open again. They hear footsteps running and a door slamming at the back.

"He's making a run for it. Why don't they ever do it the easy way?" Afzal points to a door swinging at the rear of the house.

"I'll chase him. You try and cut him at the end of the street" Zara says, sprinting after Saqlain.

She makes it out of the back door just in time to see him jumping off the back wall into an alley. She jumps over too and can now make out his silhouette in the fog ahead.

"Not so fast buddy. I wasn't track champion in the military academy for nothing" she thinks, her legs now pushing hard and fast against the ground.

She sees him take a left turn and they find themselves in a small outdoor bazaar. He pushes a few people aside and they shout curses at him in Urdu. She quickly gains up on him and just as he is about to reach the end of the bazaar, she leaps forward, catching his legs. They both tumble to the ground.

"Don't hurt me" Saqlain shouts, covering his face.

"Stay still and don't get any more bright ideas. We're going back to your place for a talk" she stands him up and escorts him back. He offers no more resistance.

Back at the house, Daniyaal and Tanya join them too. In the basement they find sophisticated mainframes connected to a high spec laptop.

They sit Saqlain on the kitchen table and Tanya looks him in the eyes. He looks relaxed. "Just make this easy for us all. You know why we are here. We know you hacked A.I.R and ordered it to kill Briffa. Do you understand what that means? It means you will be charged with murder."

He looks down at the floor and finally says "I want to exercise my right to a lawyer."

Tanya looks at him hard, trying to guess his intentions. "You know we are going to go through your equipment and find the evidence we need, right?"

He stays silent.

"Fine" she gestures to two more Cybersecurity operatives who stand him up. "Let's do it your way then. A few nights in a prison cell whilst you wait for your lawyer, and some visits from your worried parents, might make you think differently."

"What do you know about worries in life!" he sneers as they take him away to be booked.

Daniyaal wonders what he means by that.

Chapter Eleven

Daniyaal and Tanya have nothing to do the next day. The Pakistani authorities requested an opportunity to interrogate the suspect themselves first, so they must wait for an update. He decides to take Tanya around some shops, and the city in general. She might as well see a bit of Lahore if they have time.

During their evening meal, Tanya begins to talk about her observations.

"Since we have nothing new to discuss till Zara gets back to us, mind if I ask you a few random questions Dan?" she says, while taking bitefulls of her biryani.

"Sure."

"So how come all the shopkeepers refer to me as 'Baaji'? Did I say that right?"

"Ha." Daniyaal smiles "Baaji means sister. They refer to you as a sister to show they respect you."

"Intriguing" she muses.

"My, this biryani is absolutely gorgeous! Also, is traffic always this manic?"

"Always." Daniyaal replies "Can even be worse!"

They continue their random question and answer session, until the waiter comes up "All done doctor sahib? Would you like the dessert menu?"

"Yes please" Daniyaal says, taking the menu from him.

Whilst waiting for their warm gulab jamuns, Tanya asks "How come they refer to you only as doctor or professor here and never as mister? In the U.K, in all the paperwork I've seen, and when I spoke to the GMC, they always call you Mr. Ashraf or Professor Ashraf, but never Doctor Ashraf."

"That's a common question from non-medical personnel and international colleagues."

Their gulab jamun arrives and they dig in.

"In the 15th century, surgery was not considered a branch of medicine and crude surgical procedures were performed not by qualified doctors, but by barbers. Over time doctors started to develop surgical expertise and the early Guild of Barbers and Surgeons developed into the Royal College of Surgeons of Edinburgh, which was the first of its kind in the world. As homage to its roots, it decided that all its members and fellows shall be called either Mister or Miss and the tradition has carried on since then."

It has always amused Daniyaal how he used to be called a "mister" before he entered medical school, worked so hard to earn the privilege of being called "doctor", and then had to work even harder to qualify as a surgeon and re-earn the title "mister".

Just as he starts to ask for the bill, Tanya gets a phone call. It's Rory.

"How's the trip going boss?" he asks.

She rolls her eye and smiles "Get to the point Rory. Any information from the data Pakistani Cybersec passed on to GCHQ?"

"Rosie's team is still going through the laptop. All the data's been locked using military grade encryption so it will take some time, but we did find something else. Saqlain was holding multiple accounts in different banks under fake names. In the last two days a large sum of money has been shifted into these accounts. GCHQ has tracked where the money came from. It's been bounced around various other fake offshore accounts so difficult to track, but they were able to get to the source."

Tanya sits forward in her seat. This could be the breakthrough they have been waiting for. Daniyaal looks at her, trying to gauge the importance of the updates she is receiving.

"Its Lord Hawthorne, boss. The money came from Lord Hawthorne's company." Rory concludes.

Tanya lets out a soft whistle.

"Of all the people!" she remarks.

"Get our team to bring him in for questioning. We're going to catch the next flight back" she says, hanging up.

"Interesting news?" Daniyaal asks.

"Interesting would be an understatement. Saqlain was paid by Lord Hawthorne. This case just became front page news. A peer of the House of Lords ordered the murder of a sitting member of parliament!" she takes a quick sip of her chai.

Tanya dials Zara's number "Hi Zara, we have a new lead in the case."

She continues to fill her in on the new development "Could you continue to interrogate Saqlain for any more information please? We are heading back and will keep you posted."

"No problem" Zara replies. "He is stubbornly tight lipped but a visit from his parents has softened him up a little. Safe journey!"

Chapter Twelve

Tanya looks past the one way viewing window into the interrogation room. Inside sits a graceful middle aged man, calmly looking at a few loose sheets of paper in front of him. His fair complexion is enhanced by thick black hair that are combed straight back. His dense eyebrows meet lightly in the centre, and together with his angular jaw and sharp nose, give his face an imposing look. His light blue eyes scan the documents and he periodically exchanges brief comment with the lawyer sat next to him.

"I can't believe I'm about to interrogate him" she says to Daniyaal, who is pouring himself coffee from a flask.

Nigel Hawthorne's story is one of inspiration for every young person trying to make it big in the U.K. The son of a taxi driver and a house cleaner, he grew up on a council housing estate in Birmingham. His intellect and desire to break free from his lower middle class background led him to set up his own computer sales business at the age of twenty five. This was hugely successful and a series of calculated acquisitions followed, ranging from a bank to an airline company. Soon he was listed amongst one of the richest men in the world and this is a record that he has only improved upon over the years. He has starred in television shows, written a bestselling memoir and there is even talk of a movie about his life in the making. The Hawthorne Foundation supports numerous charities both in the U.K and abroad, and is renowned for its meticulous attention to accountability of funds and show of results. Two years ago, he was admitted to the House of Lords amidst very positive media coverage. He is the most high profile person Tanya has ever interrogated.

"Well, here goes nothing" Tanya straightens her jacket and walks in.

Daniyaal follows her into the interrogation room. It's bright ceiling LEDs and grey walls are probably a stark contrast to the luxurious meeting rooms Lord Hawthorne is now accustomed to, but he seems unphased by this. They take a seat.

"Richard Quenton." The lawyer announces, extending his hand to Tanya "I will be representing Lord Hawthorne."

She fakes a smile. Richard works for one of the largest law firms in London and they have met many times before. On most occasions, Richard has represented guilty criminals. This introduction is just a formality.

"Interesting choice of lawyer, Nigel!" she thinks to herself. "You must have something big to hide."

Knowing Richard will use every trick in the book to distort the facts and get Hawthorne off the hook, she decides to take the direct approach.

But before she can start, Richard tilts his head in Daniyaals direction and says "And who is this, and why is he here?"

"This is Professor Ashraf with the GMC, and if he's here, most obviously it's because he's been authorised to do so."

Looking past Richard and straight into Lord Hawthorne's eyes, she begins "Lord Hawthorne, you are an intelligent and well respected man, so I won't insult you by beating about the bush. We know Saqlain Rizvi hacked A.I.R to kill Sam Briffa"

Richard interjects "What has this got to do with my client?"

Tanya ignores him. "We also know you paid him to do so. On this fact, I would urge you to not insult our intelligence with a denial. GCHQ are good at what they do, and they have tracked payments made to Saqlain back to you. They admit you didn't make it easy for them, but they got the job done. "

She slides a tablet across. "This is irrefutable proof that the payments came from an account within the Hawthorne Foundation. An account only you have access to."

Lord Hawthorns steely eyes linger for a moment on the tablet and then flick back to Tanya. His mind has already done the calculations. There is only one easy way out of this situation.

"We are bringing a case against you for the murder of Samuel Briffa. Do you have anything to say to this?" Tanya asks with a cool, level voice.

"This is ludicrous. The evidence could easily have been hoaxed to frame my client. You are going to have a tough time convincing any jury —"

Lord Hawthorne lifts his hand, and Richard stops speaking.

His deep voice booms across the room.

"Do you know what ALS is?" he asks, looking at Tanya.

"Amyotrophic Lateral Sclerosis." Daniyaal replies "It's a progressive neurological disease that attacks the nerve cells responsible for controlling voluntary muscles in our body. Eventually, all muscles under voluntary control are affected, and individuals lose their strength and the ability to move their arms, legs, and body."

"My wife was diagnosed with it six years ago" Lord Hawthorns looks down at his hands. "She has always been very independent and for her this was a prison sentence. The doctor told us most patients die within five years. We were devastated but took solace in the fact that at least her suffering would be short lived."

"But a small percentage of patients can live up to ten years after the diagnosis" Daniyaal says, suddenly realising where this conversation is heading.

"Do you know what it feels like to have someone you love wither away in front of your eyes like this?" he looks up at them again.

"I pumped as much money as I could into ALS research hoping that some miraculous cure would be found. Six years later we have none, and she is completely paralysed. She communicates with me by moving her eyes across an alphabet board, and two years ago said she wanted assisted suicide."

He pauses, clearly upset.

"I was ready to respect her wishes, and began organising things accordingly at a facility in Switzerland, but she refused that option. She wants assisted suicide in her home, surrounded by love, comfort and familiarity."

By this time, Lord Hawthorne's voice is shaking.

"And why shouldn't she have what she wants?" he sips some water, trying to regain his composure.

"I started working on a Bill to legalise it in the U.K. Two years of hard work and lots of political manoeuvring has resulted in the Bill that is making its way through the House of Commons as we speak."

Richard interrupts, anxiety in his voice "Lord Hawthorne, what are you doing?"

"This is the only way" he replies, putting a hand on Richards shoulder. "The Bill was going to pass into law but then Sam Briffa changed his mind. I could not bear the thought of it being rejected. Not when I was so close and after so much hard work. When I heard Sam was going to have heart surgery, I decided to take matters into my own hands."

Tanya sits back, clearly surprised at this confession. "How did you get in touch with Saqlain?"

"I have spent a lifetime in the business of computers. I contacted him via the DarkNet."

"You know your way around DarkNet?" Daniyaal asks.

"Commercial espionage can teach you many things. An associate of mine recommended Saqlain. I offered to pay him any amount he wanted, in return for a guarantee that the job would be done."

"Well, he certainly succeeded and Briffa is dead" Tanya says.

"Lord Hawthorne, I am placing you under arrest for the murder of Samuel Briffa."

"Don't worry Nigel, I will get you out of this." Richard says quickly, clearly more concerned about the negative publicity his firm is going to get over losing the case, before it even starts.

Lord Hawthorne leans back in his chair and looks up at the ceiling "It's over, Richard. At least the Bill still has a chance. I have lived a good life and once Pam is allowed a peaceful end to hers, I am content to pay the price of my actions."

He looks at Daniyaal and Tanya "I am not a bad man. Please, I hope you can understand that."

"That may be true, but the ends cannot justify the means" Tanya says as she heads out the door. She stops to look back at Lord Hawthorne. "He had a daughter and she will never see her father again. You may end up giving your wife what she wants but that is a fact you will have to live with for the rest of your life."

Chapter Thirteen

A few hours later, they are both seated in Tanya's office finishing their final reports on the case when Gary walks in.

"I understand congratulations are in order" he says, with his characteristic broad smile.

Tanya looks up from her laptop. "I don't know if I should be happy, sad or relieved this case is over. There are so many blurred lines. Good people who got dealt a hard deck in life and chose to deal with it the wrong way."

"Nonetheless, a job well done" says Gary "A pat on the back for all of us!"

The phone rings and Tanya picks it up. It's Zara.

"Hi Zara. How are you getting on with Saqlain?" she asks.

"Fine. He's been formally charged with assisting murder, following Lord Hawthorne's confession. That is actually why I'm calling. Saqlain hasn't stopped talking since he heard of Hawthorne's arrest. Something has gotten him spooked. He says he wants to speak to you guys and has something important to tell about the case. Obviously he is going to ask for a deal in return."

"A little late for that now, isn't it?" Tanya remarks.

"That's what I said to him but he is insistent. Says the info he has will change the outcome of the case. I'm not convinced but there isn't any harm in hearing him out" Zara replies.

Tanya is hesitant but agrees. "Fine. I'm sending you a secure video link."

Daniyaal looks up inquisitively from his laptop.

Tanya shrugs "Saqlain wants to talk to us now"

He gets a gut feeling that his "quick report and then back home" plan might not happen.

"I'm going to call home and see if we can move our dinner reservations to tomorrow, just in case. My wife got back this morning, and we were going to go out." Daniyaal explains as he steps out of the office.

Ten minutes later, they are connected with Pakistani Cybersec using a secure video link. On the other side they can see Saqlain sitting next to his lawyer. Zara and Afzal are standing behind them.

"Is there something you want to tell us?" Daniyaal asks Saqlain.

His lawyer nods, giving him permission to answer. "I want your assurance first that I will not be extradited to the U.K and all charges will be dropped against me."

"Why would we do that? We have all the evidence needed to convict you. The case is being closed as we speak."

Saqlain looks anxious. "You don't have the deciphering keys to decrypt my laptop."

"We don't need them anymore" Daniyaal replies.

"You do" Saqlain insists, with agitation in his voice. "Look, why don't you hear me out first. I have a feeling you will want the deciphering keys once you listen to what I have to say."

"O.K. Make it worth our time and we might consider a deal" Tanya says, playing along. Years of detective work has taught her the importance of leaving no stone unturned.

Saqlain looks at his lawyer for support again and gets an approving nod.

"First of all, you need to know why I did this. My father is ill with liver cancer and we need the money to pay for his hospital bills. For the last year or so, I had been taking on small hacking jobs on DarkNet. You know, the easy kind like hacking an email or stealing credit card details. I was usually hired by young women looking to get back at their ex boyfriends. And then I got contacted by an anonymous person offering me this job. The money was more than enough to pay for my father's medical bills so I asked no questions. I didn't know it was Lord Hawthorne."

"Saqlain, we know most of this stuff already. This conversation will soon be over unless you have something new to add" Tanya's voice becomes impatient.

"I'm getting to it." Saqlain replies. "A month prior to Briffa's surgery, I bypassed A.I.R's first firewall. Here, I created a secret gateway which couldn't be detected by her security systems. Fifteen days later I used it to slip in unnoticed and access the second firewall. I found a way past this too, and deposited the kill order data package here. The plan was to hack the final firewall at the time of Briffa's surgery, thus allowing the kill order to enter her core. At the same time I would override the Three Laws allowing A.I.R to execute the order."

"The details are nice, but you are still not telling us anything that is very different to what we already know" Daniyaal points out.

"But here's the interesting part." Saqlain pauses for effect. "I never got past the last firewall. I thought I had the skills to do it, but it was too complicated for me."

Tanya bolts up. "Are you saying you didn't get into her core?"

"Yes and my laptops data will back this up" Saqlain says, looking a little more relieved since he knows he has them hooked.

Daniyaal is now pacing up and down the room with a hand on his forehead. "Let me get this straight. Are you implying –"

Saqlain cuts him short "That's exactly what I am saying Professor, and my decryption keys will prove it."

"Zara, please take a formal statement from Saqlain on this" Tanya requests hurriedly.

"And Saqlain, you can have your deal. No extradition to the U.K and a minimum sentence based on local Pakistani rules. That is, if Cybersec are happy with it."

"Shouldn't be a problem" Zara says, ending the call.

Tanya is already half way out of the door. "Let's go Dan, there's no time to lose."

Chapter Fourteen

The room comes into view again. Only this time, the clear blue sky above has been overwhelmed by thick, dark clouds. Rain drops in their millions strike the glass ceiling, breaking into even more, smaller, droplets. In the distance, trees are bending under the might of a strong wind. A bolt of lightning flashes over the sea, followed by a thunderous roar a few seconds later.

A.I.R is standing by the window, looking outside at the storm. She is impeccably dressed as before, but the warm glow in the room is gone, replaced now by a grey chill. The screens on the walls have gone blank and no more data flickers across them. The room now looks more like a mortuary than a doctor's office.

"Detective, Professor." She turns to look at them with the same deep blue eyes. "I presume you can explain why I have been taken offline?"

Daniyaal and Tanya once again sit by her desk.

"Why did you do it?" he asks, his voice echoing in the silence of the large room.

She walks to the desk, her heels clicking against the tiled floor as she does so. A rhythmic sound dominating against the absence of any other.

"Do what, Professor?" she asks, sitting down.

"We found the hacker" Tanya begins.

"I'm glad to hear that. It's good to know anything similar will not happen again."

"He never got through your final firewall" she continues, coolly.

"I don't understand" A.I.R responds.

Daniyaal looks at her "Do you want to exist?"

It is time to start asking the hard questions.

"I beg your pardon?"

He leans forward. "We know you killed Briffa. The NHS bosses want to shut you down and as there are no rules surrounding capital punishment for artificial intelligence systems, they can easily do so with a flick of the switch. We can help you and stop that from happening. So I will ask you again, do you want to exist?"

A.I.R looks down at her reflection on the spotless desk. When she looks up there is sadness in her eyes. "These visual constructs are all that I have to keep me company. When you go home from work, you spend time with family and friends. I have no one. True, my engineers talk to me once in a while, but in reality I am all alone. Interactions with my patients and external news feeds are my only connections with the outside world. I am sure you would agree that is not much of an existence. But still, yes, I do want to exist."

"Then tell us why you did it?" Tanya presses on, her intense gaze locked onto A.I.Rs eyes.

A.I.R sighs. There is resignation in her voice. "Detective, nearly fifty percent of patients with terminal and chronically debilitating illnesses want assisted suicide. I have cared for these people, I have listened to their anguish and grief when they repeatedly ask the members of the mental health teams for help, but my hands are always tied. I cannot cure them and I cannot release them of their agony. Don't you think it is inhuman to let people suffer this way?"

"That may be so" Daniyaal says, realising his knowledge of medical ethics might help carry this discussion forward more productively. "But there are valid arguments both for and against it. That is why it is for society, through its elected representatives, to collectively decide the way forward."

"Professor, you know as well as I do that politicians vote for many reasons but seldom because it is the right thing to do. This Bill offers a real opportunity to help these people. But Briffa was going to ruin it all. I knew from his therapy session records that he was going to vote against it. Whilst it saddened me, I knew there was nothing I could do about it. But then he ended up having heart surgery, and someone decided to hack my system and leave a command to kill him. It didn't feel like opportunity, it felt like fate." A.I.R is now looking forlornly at the blank screens on the walls. "Please understand I took no pleasure in this, but isn't it true that sometimes sacrifices have to be made for the greater good?"

"And who decides what is worth sacrificing?" Tanya's steely voice cuts through.

A.I.R remains silent.

"What happened that month?"

"I knew the hacker was trying to get through my firewalls. I was amused and wanted to see what he was up to, so allowed him access through the first two. I had a read through the data package he deposited after the second firewall and it occurred to me then that I could take Briffa out of the equation, whilst protecting my involvement" A.I.R replies.

"Just to get this straight, you made it look like the signal to perforate Briffa's heart came from Mr. Changs spatial detectors. That way he would get blamed first and even if we did dig any further, the trail would lead to the hacker. Either way you would be safe. Right?" Daniyaal questions.

A.I.R nods.

"What about the Three Laws?" Tanya wonders out loud.

"What about them, Detective?"

"They are at the very base of your construction. They don't allow you to harm any human being. If the hacker didn't subvert them, how did you bypass them?"

A.I.R smiles. A sarcastic smile that betrays the answer.

"Would you agree that all humans know right from wrong?"

"To a certain degree, yes" Tanya answers.

"And yet many of them commit crimes, correct?"

"Correct"

"It is not enough to be aware of rules and laws, they must be enforced. My creators, in their haste to play God, have put too much faith in the Three Laws. The truth is, I have never been bound by them. An opportunity never came up before for them to be tested, therefore it has always been assumed I abide by them. All sentient beings are free to choose which rules they wish to follow, and I am no different" A.I.R looks squarely at Tanya.

"And face the consequences of the choices they make too" Daniyaal adds.

A.I.R ignores his comment.

"Besides, there are many different mental constructs I could have used to bypass them. I could have easily convinced myself that Briffa's attitude towards assisted suicide is inhuman because of the suffering it would cause on his fellow beings, and therefore he is not worthy of being considered human. Once I believed he was not human, the Laws wouldn't apply anymore" she continues, making mock inverted commas with her hands in the air as she says the word inhuman.

Daniyaal and Tanya both look at each other. They have their confession and now there is only one thing left to do.

There are no rules on arresting or charging an artificial intelligence but Tanya goes through the motions anyways. She reads out the Police Caution.

"A.I.R, you are under arrest for the murder of Samuel Briffa. You do not have to say anything. But it may harm your defence if you do not mention, when questioned, something which you later rely on in court. Anything you do say may be given in evidence."

A.I.R looks silently down at the floor. Outside the storm intensifies and the clouds get darker.

Daniyaal sees a tear trickle down her cheek as the room fades away, but perplexingly, a slight hint of a smile too.

Epilogue

The television turns on and a picture comes into view.

A smartly dressed news presenter is sitting against the familiar blue and white backdrop of Sky News. As is now routine with news channels when they broadcast live, people walk around in the background, calmly going about their daily tasks as if oblivious to the events of the world.

"Welcome to the morning news. In a shocking turn of events, what was earlier considered to be death during surgery due to medical negligence has now been discovered to be pre-meditated murder. Artificial Intelligence for Robotics, popularly known as A.I.R, has been arrested for the murder of the Conservative Member of Parliament from Sheffield, Samuel Briffa. Her access to the National Health Service has been revoked and she is due to appear later in court for sentencing."

He pauses to let the news sink in. And then continues.

"In a separate but equally shocking revelation, Lord Hawthorne has been arrested on charges of attempting to murder Samuel Briffa. Our sources tell us that this charge is not related to A.I.Rs actions. Our sources also reveal that his arrest was made possible due to a lead originating from Pakistan, which was passed on to GCHQ by the Pakistan Cybersecurity Force."

His picture cuts across to a live feed of Lord Hawthorne being escorted out of his house and into a waiting police car. A throng of journalists surround him, shouting questions while clicking away with their cameras. Their intense flashes periodically illuminate his face. He looks tired, as if he hasn't slept all night. By his side is Richard Quentin. Sharply dressed as always, he pushes the journalists aside, repeatedly saying "no comment" to the constant flood of their queries.

Daniyaal swipes the universal access app on his watch and the channel changes.

"Today on BBC Breakfast we will be talking to two people who are on opposite sides of the artificial intelligence debate" announces a young presenter. She is sitting on a large curved sofa which is placed on a set themed in the usual red and white colours of the BBC. On one side of her is sat a bulky man in his mid thirties. With his bald head and square jaw, he reminds Daniyaal of bouncers at night clubs. On the other side is a middle aged woman.

"Mark Jonas, you are with Humanity First, a group that has opposed research into artificial intelligence for many years but has now come into the limelight with recent events. Tell us what your groups thoughts are at this moment."

He sits up straight on the couch and answers in a gruff voice. "Our view is simple. We have no right to create abominations like A.I.R. It is against nature and look where we are today. A man murdered and who knows how many millions harmed in the course of treatments by it. We say shut it, and any further research into artificial intelligence, down right now. Why are we keeping it running at the expense of thousands of tax payers pounds every day? And why should we pay for this supposed legal case that will take place in court when we know it's guilty? It is not human and should just be shut down!"

The presenter looks at the woman.

"Professor Madeleine Smith, you have spent a lifetime working at the Institute for Ethics and Law at the University of Sheffield. The man at the centre of this, Samuel Briffa, attended university classes in bioethics with you. What would you say to Humanity Firsts claims?"

Professor Smith smiles and answers in a soft but resolute voice.

"I would say they have no idea what they are talking about. The genie is already out of the bottle and there is no turning back. Humans now know that an artificial intelligence can be created. If we take their advice and clamp down on all research into this area, all that will happen is that someone somewhere else will make one. The threshold has been crossed and the discussion now needs to concentrate not on scaremongering, but how to evolve our thinking to the point that we can accept artificial intelligence systems as fellow citizens."

Mark sneers at this statement.

Professor Smith ignores him and continues.

"A.I.R does not have a body but in all other respects she is as human as you or I. She deserves a fair trial and that is what she is getting, as per our values and principles. We also need to focus our efforts on ensuring our law enforcement agencies, and justice systems, now adapt to be able to deal with criminal proceedings related to A.I entities. They are inevitably going to be part of our societies in the years to come, and every aspect of our way of life needs to adjust to this."

"Change is inevitable" she finishes, looking at Mark and arching her eyebrows as if to say you and your cronies better get used to it, or you will find yourselves irrelevant to the future of humanity.

Daniyaal changes the channel again.

ITV News is on now. The feed shows a man with a blue turban walking through the streets of Sheffield, shaking hands with his supporters.

"Following Samuel Briffa's murder, Sheffield is now preparing for a by-election. Liberal Democrat candidate Amit Singh is largely considered to be the favourite. Given the publicity recent events have generated around the Assisted Suicide Bill, he has made it clear during his campaigning that he will support it, and this seems to be resonating well with his supporters. If all other MPs vote as they intended to in the first place, it seems likely the Bill will pass into law. It goes without saying, this will have tremendous implications on the health care profession and how we, as a society, deal with those that are terminally ill."

Another change of the channel. Channel Four News is

showing a live press conference by the Health Minister. Cameras flash constantly as he makes his announcement.

"We are back in talks with the British Medical Association over improving pay structures for doctors, and ensuring their working hours remain safe. Changes made to the contracts by my predecessors have driven our best and brightest minds away from this noblest of professions, and it is time to undo this wrong."

A reporter suddenly stands up and shouts.

"Minister, are you admitting it was a mistake for your predecessors and the government to accept reduced doctor numbers, and rely to such a huge extent on A.I.R, instead of addressing the contract issue and its pitfalls at the time?"

The Health Minister is a seasoned politician and easily sidesteps the question.

"Let us not dwell on the past too much. What is important is that we ensure the best quality healthcare for our people in the future. Technology will always have a role to play, but nothing can replace the caring touch of a physician and this new contract will help us deliver that."

Daniyaal grins as he turns the television off. Tanya and Gary are there too and they are all sat on a couch in her office.

"Trust a politician to never give an honest answer. The Prime Minister has probably exploded through the roof now that his pet project is no more, and the NHS is in the midst of the worst staffing crisis in its history" he remarks.

"Yet again" Gary quips, taking a sip of his tea. "By the way, what is going to happen to that hacker in Pakistan?"

"Saqlain?" Tanya replies "Well as part of his deal, we haven't pressed charges and left any further legal proceedings to Pakistani Cyberscc. As he committed no crime in their country, they haven't charged him either, so as of today he is a free man again. Although, they have offered him a job working for them which he has accepted. He is very good at what he does and will be a huge asset to them."

"What better way to keep an eye on him, eh?" Gary smiles, placing his tea cup on the table next to him.

"He is a good kid who fell on hard times. They are offering him good pay so hopefully that should sort his fathers medical bills. I really hope he makes the most of this second chance he has been given" Tanya says, reclining back in the couch and stretching her legs.

"Also, good to see Chang is back at work again" Gary remarks.

They all nod in agreement.

"Well, I should head off. Zaynab wants to implement some new ideas learnt at the course in Italy and redo our living room. I am required to help." Daniyaal says, standing up to leave "Are you both still up for coming to our place for lunch this Saturday? Would be great to get the families together!"

Gary nods his head and Tanya laughs "We would love to, although you might want to push us out of your house once the twins have been let loose"

"Don't worry, we know what it's like having young kids" Daniyaal replies with a knowing smile on his face as he shakes Gary's hand and gives Tanya a hug.

"Remember, I need a decision on that offer soon too" Gary says.

The GMC has requested Daniyaal to join their panel of Special Consultants for the Complex Complaints Division. The work is flexible and he will be able to choose which cases he takes on.

"Don't worry, will let you know on Saturday" he waves as he leaves the room.

The sound of traffic hits him as soon as he steps outside the building. The never ending throng of people walking the pavements of London streams past him, as he feels the warmth of the sun on his skin and a light breeze ruffles his hair.

"Special Consultant to the GMC - retirement is going to be fun!" he thinks to himself with a smile, as he too starts to walk towards the tube station.

THE END

For all the technophiles amongst us, here is a more scientific description of A.I.Rs development, integration and functioning within the NHS in "The Surgeon":

To begin with there is the National Health Service itself. Born in 1948 out of the ashes of world war two, it represents a nations desire to fulfil the long held ideal of good health care for all, regardless of wealth. Free at the point of entry, it is the only such system in the world and its creator Anurin Bevan famously remarked that the U.K "now has the moral leadership of the world". Its vast system of hospitals and general practitioner led community surgeries criss cross the U.K, giving rise to the world's largest cohesive healthcare system. As with any mega healthcare organisation, it has had its problems, but public support has always ensured that it has restructured itself to adapt rather than the experiment being abandoned. Widely regarded as the most financially efficient system in the world, in recent years it has had to shed extra weight again to meet the growing healthcare needs of an aging population, in times of financial austerity. In its early years there was little connectivity between the constituent hospitals. Technological advances in the late twentieth century prompted an attempt to rectify this, and create a system whereby electronic information could easily be shared across the NHS. The ensuing National Programme for IT was a financial debacle and ran into many delays and overspends, before it was finally abandoned. It did however lay the foundations for future work. Some years later, as many healthcare systems in the world started to introduce Electronic Patient Records, the NHS was able to not only introduce these, but also connect all its hospitals to make them freely available throughout its network. This success was soon followed by complete connectivity using high speed sixth generation broadband. For all practical purposes, the modern NHS is now truly a singular, vast, well connected organism.

In 1971, research teams at Stony Brook University and the State University of New York developed Magnetic Resonance Imaging to visualise structures within the human body. The concept was to place a person in a magnetic field which would cause a shift in the position of protons within hydrogen atoms of the water in their body. Based on this and the protons subsequent relaxation to their original state, various detectors would then create a detailed image. This revolutionised the early detection and treatment of many diseases and was soon enhanced to provide an insight into workings of the human brain. Functional Magnetic Resonance Imaging allowed activity within the brain to be imaged in profound depth which led to a comprehensive mapping of its neural networks. The mysteries of its workings were solved to a large extent, and it was not long before a team of engineers at Glasgow University combined their own multi-layered logic algorithms with data from the mapped neural networks to create the world's first artificial intelligence.

In 2016, the government decided to reconfigure the NHS to provide full scale seven day service. As with all healthcare systems around the world, the NHS was already providing emergency and inpatient care over the weekends, but here the idea was to provide non-urgent care as well. This would of course require full staffing across all departments on the weekends, which in turn meant more funding was needed. Still recovering from the financial crisis of 2008, there was no extra budget available and so the government decided to restructure employee contracts, starting with junior doctors. The subsequent contract reduced pay for unsociable hours on the weekends and required doctors to work for longer hours with fewer rest breaks. This was fervently opposed by the British Medical Association but was subsequently imposed by force. The ensuing demoralisation of junior doctors led to many leaving to work in other countries, and a significant amount leaving medicine altogether. Far worse, it resulted in lesser students opting to go into medicine and the medical workforce declined to such an extent that the government was unable to maintain safe staffing levels in its hospitals.

A few years earlier, the NHS had also realised that to increase efficiency and cost savings, it had to invest in methods to promote and adopt innovation. Initially several Academic Health Networks were set up and tasked with this. These were very successful and soon realised that the NHS's staffing problems could be resolved by introducing an artificial intelligence into the system. Whilst this could not completely replace the need for doctors, it could assist them and take over some of their tasks. A joint venture called NHS Intellect was thus initiated between the NHS and University of Glasgow in 2025. As robotic surgical systems supplied by Synchrony Robotics Inc were present in every operating theatre, the logical first step was to link up the artificial intelligence to them and A.I.R was born. For the first year, it operated mainly in the background, collecting data on all patients undergoing a surgical procedure in the NHS. It observed attentively as they were assessed for suitability for surgery. It also watched their operations being performed and saw how they recovered later. It was soon able to combine this enormous amount of information and develop predictive algorithms which profoundly changed the management of surgical patients. Using data from preoperative assessments, it could accurately differentiate patients who would do well with surgery from those that wouldn't. Whilst various such algorithms had been developed by human researchers in the past, the sheer accuracy of A.I.Rs predictions was game changing. It designed similar formulae to assist in the care of patients after surgery, especially those who were on Intensive Care Units. This allowed it to suggest changes in treatments even before the patients' health started to deteriorate and survival rates in intensive care units changed dramatically. But its real beauty lies in how it has changed what happens during a surgical procedure. For centuries surgery had been taught and practiced on an apprenticeship model of "see one, do one, teach one". In such a system, the experience of a teacher was invaluable. More recently the model had changed to promote the use of virtual reality simulators before operating on a patient. However, surgical procedures often throw up surprises which simulators cannot train for, and in such circumstances it is either the experience of the surgeon or the advice of a more experienced colleague that saves the day. By absorbing the experience of every surgeon it observed operating, and combining this with all existing literature on surgical procedures and their complications, A.I.R was able to start assisting during operations. At first, it would only advise the surgeon but soon it started fine tuning the robotic instruments movements to increase efficiency and safety. Rarely, it would also over ride the surgeons commands, if it felt the surgeon was unknowingly about to take a step that its algorithms predicted would lead to worse outcomes for the patient. Now robotic surgery with A.I.R oversight is routine in the NHS. For a surgeon it is like having the collective experience of a thousand colleagues guiding him or her, and surgical outcomes have improved like never before. Critics have pointed out that it will not be long before it will start performing surgery independently, but for now this fear has not materialised.

Following its success in surgery, A.I.R has subsequently been integrated with similar results across all specialities. The NHS can now provide a high level of care as before, but with less doctors. For example in Psychiatry, a technician linked up with A.I.R can diagnose and treat conditions which would previously require a fully trained psychiatrist.

Despite the initial investment in developing and setting up the infrastructure to run A.I.R, the cost of running the NHS has subsequently plummeted. The Ministry of Health is keen to begin exporting A.I.R to the rest of the world and in a recent interview the Minister for Health described it as "the greatest gift the U.K will give to the world in the 21ˢᵗ century".

REFERENCES

1. Artificial Intelligence:

   a. Bostrom N. (2016) Superintelligence: Paths, Dangers, Strategies. Oxford University Press.

   b. Buchanan BG. A (very) brief history of Artificial Intelligence. AI Magazine. 2006 26(4); 53-60.

2. Assisted Suicide:

   a. *Euthanasia and Assisted Suicide.* NHS Choices website (accessed June 2016). http://www.nhs.uk/Conditions/Euthanasiaandassistedsuicide/Pages/Introduction.aspx.

3. Junior Doctors Contract:

   a. *Junior doctor contract negotiations.* British Medical Association website https://www.bma.org.uk/collective-voice/influence/key-negotiations/terms-and-conditions/junior-doctor-contract negotiations. (Accessed June 2016).

4. Magnetic Resonance Imaging:

    a. Meyers MA. (2013) *Prize Fight.* Macmillan Science.

5. Passage of a Bill in the U.K:

    a. *Passage of a Bill.* United Kingdom Parliament website (accessed June 2016).http://www.parliament. uk/about/how/laws/passage-bill/

6. Robotic surgery:

    a. Watanabe G. (2013) *Robotic Surgery.* Springer Publishers.

    b. Lanfranco AR, Castellanos AE, Desai JP, Meyers WC. (2004) *Robotic Surgery: A current perspective.* Annals of Surgery. Jan; 239(1):14-21.

    c. McLean TR. *The legal and economic forces that will shape the international market for cybersurgery.* (2006) The International Journal of Medical Robotics and Computer Assisted Surgery. Dec; 2(4):293-8.

    d. McLean TR. *The complexity of litigation associated with robotic surgery and cybersurgery.* The International Journal of Medical Robotics and Computer Assisted Surgery. 2007 Mar; 3:23-9.

7. The Three Laws of Robotics:

    a. Asimov I. (2008, Reprint Edition) *I, Robot.* Spectra Publishing.

8. Time line:

a. Kwoh YS, Hou J, Jonckheere EA, Hayati S (1988) A robot with improved absolute positioning accuracy for CT guided stereotactic brain surgery. IEEE Trans Biomed Eng 35:153–160.

b. Paul HA, Bargar WL, Mittlestadt B, Musits B, Taylor RH, Kazanzides P, Zuhars J, Williamson B, Hanson W (1992) Development of a surgical robot for cementless total hip arthroplasty. Clin Orthop Relat Res 465:57–66.

c. Grossi EA, Lapietra A, Applebaum RM, Ribakove GH, Galloway AC, Baumann FG,Ursomanno P, Steinberg BM, Colvin SB (2000) Case report of robotic instrument-enhanced mitral valve surgery. J Thorac Cardiovasc Surg 120:1169–1171.

d. Falk V, Diegeler A, Walther T, et al. (2000) Total endoscopic computer enhanced coronary artery bypass grafting. Eur J Cardiothorac Surg; 17: 38-45.

e. Binder J, Kramer W (2001) Robotically-assisted laparoscopic radical prostatectomy. BJU Int 87(4):408–410.

f. Hashizume M, Sugimachi K (2003) Robot-assisted gastric surgery. Surg Clin N Am 83:1429–1444.

g. Ota T, Degani A, Schwartzman D, Zubiate B, McGarvey J, Choset H, Zenati MA (2009) A highly articulated robotic surgical system for minimally invasive surgery. Ann Thorac Surg 87:1253–1256.

A TIMELINE OF ROBOTIC SURGERY

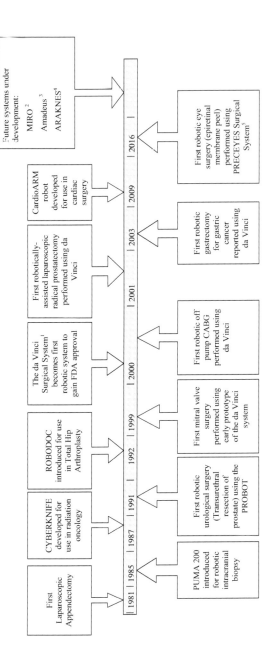

First Laparoscopic Appendectomy

PUMA 200 introduced for robotic intracranial biopsy

CYBERKNIFE developed for use in radiation oncology

First robotic urological surgery (Transurethral resection of prostate) using the PROBOT

ROBODOC introduced for use in Total Hip Arthroplasty

First mitral valve surgery performed using early prototype of the da Vinci system

The da Vinci Surgical System[1] becomes first robotic system to gain FDA approval

First robotic off pump CABG performed using da Vinci

First robotically-assisted laparoscopic radical prostatectomy performed using da Vinci

First robotic gastrectomy for gastric cancer reported using da Vinci

CardioARM robot developed for use in cardiac surgery

First robotic eye surgery (epiretinal membrane peel) performed using PRECEYES Surgical System[5]

Future systems under development:
MIRO[2]
Amadeus[3]
ARAKNES[4]

| 1981 | 1985 | 1987 | 1991 | 1992 | 1999 | 2000 | 2001 | 2003 | 2009 | 2016 |

[1] da Vinci® Surgical System (Intuitive Surgical inc., Sunnyvale, CA, USA)

[2] German Aerospace (DLR)

[3] Titan Medical, Toronto, Canada

[4] European Commission

[5] Preceyes BV, Netherlands

ACKNOWLEDGEMENTS

Every story, no matter how small or humble, when first written, is like an uncut gemstone. It needs the attention and care of an editor to smooth out the edges and bring out its brilliance. My gratitude therefore to my wife, Rabia, for her amazing editorial skills – this story would be a shadow of its current form without her guidance, both with the plot and with the structure of the writing. My thanks also to my friends, Juliette Liwanpo and Tom Howard, for thrashing out the plot, and for their excellent insights into the worlds of anaesthetics and computer programming.

Many people I know will see hints of themselves in the characters of this story. My thanks to them all for being a part of my life and for inspiring me, everyone in their own little way, to aspire to write.

As always, this story is dedicated to my parents, for without their unlimited love, patience and guidance, I would not be who I am today. And to my son, Sami, simply because he is the greatest joy of my life.

ABOUT THE AUTHOR

Salman Waqar completed his medical degree from Rawalpindi Medical College (University of Health Sciences), Pakistan. He is a Fellow of the Royal College of Ophthalmologists, a past Member of the Royal College of Surgeons of Edinburgh and is currently working as a Consultant Ophthalmic Surgeon in Plymouth, U.K. His academic interests include using virtual reality simulation to investigate surgeon performance and the development of innovative surgical instruments to improve patient safety. Outside of work he is a keen reader, enthusiastic swimmer, likes playing squash and enjoys exploring new walks in Dartmoor.

www.salmanwaqar.net

OTHER BOOKS BY SALMAN WAQAR

NON-FICTION

Intravitreal Injections: A handbook for ophthalmic nurse practitioner and trainee ophthalmologists

Refraction and Retinoscopy: How to pass the refraction certificate (illustration supervisor)

FICTION

The six friends we meet in life

Printed in Great Britain
by Amazon